Where the Crawdads Sing

Delia Owens

ISBN 9781089379171

This book is a work of fiction. Names, characters and incidents are the product of the author's imagination. Any resemblance to actual persons, living or dead is entirely coincidental.

Davenport and other locations mentioned in this book are actual locations in Iowa. As stated, this novel is a work of fiction and no such murder has ever occurred on the bike path or in Buffalo, Iowa.

BONES

Dice don't lie . . . or do they?

JOHN F. GILL

Dedicated to my mom, Viola Gill

In her mid-80's she wrote her first book and inspired me to dip my pen into the world of unbridled imagination.

Prologue

For those unfamiliar with gambling lore, BONES refers to dice as in "Roll Dem Bones." Bones is also the handle for a killer who stalks the streets of Davenport, Iowa.

"If you don't stop crying, I'll flush you down the toilet and you can play with the rats all day."

Auntie Annabelle paid for her sins, but was it enough to flush the demons from the mind of a traumatized young man?

CHAPTER 1

Tuesday, July 6th Davenport, Iowa

The twin-rusted hinges aired a piercing screech as a willowy female hand pushed open the screened porch door. Equally annoying was the booming sound it made as it slammed shut against the weathered door jam.

Tillie Silvermann's eyes narrowed to mere slivers as her head dropped down between her upraised shoulders and her hands flashed to her reddened face. At 5:45 A.M the other renters were not pleased with her early morning wake-up calls. When she returned, she'd probably have to deal with another nasty note from the old biddy down the hall.

Twelve steps led down to the sidewalk which she took two at a time, pausing momentarily at the bottom to decide which direction she would take. She chose to go right, which would lead her to Davenport, Iowa's, Duck Creek

Recreational Trail, a 13.5-mile trek. Perfect for an early morning run.

Even before reaching the turnoff, sweat snaked down her forehead and back, stinging her eyes and soaking the clothes that clung tightly to her athletic five-foot six-inch frame. The cool of the night did nothing to halt the past week's record-breaking temperatures and high humidity, but that was okay. Tillie thrived in this type of weather.

Her strides were long and effortless as she turned onto the trail twelve blocks from home. Tillie checked her Fitbit and was pleased with her time. However, if she wanted to win the seven mile Bix road race later in the month she needed to pick up the pace. So, with little effort, she changed gears and raced west towards Emeis Golf Course.

Her muscles, like the strings of a Stradivarius, were orchestrated to perfection by its master. Her cheeks puffed out as she exhaled the oxygen-deprived air. Truly a gorgeous day for her early morning run.

As Tillie rounded a bend, she noticed a groundhog stick his nose out of its burrow and sniff the morning air. Spotting Tillie, he lowered his furry, russet body back into his hole, but kept a vigilant eye on this early morning intruder.

Tillie slowed to a jog, then stopped completely. She pulled her I-Phone from her fanny pack and snapped a couple of pictures. Foregoing her morning run, she stepped off the bike path and chose to rest on a grassy knoll. She loved her early morning routine, and nature as well.

To her left, two squirrels played tag...one brown, the other black. They danced around one of the many ancient oaks that graced the bike path. She had never seen a black squirrel before moving to Davenport and couldn’t pass up the opportunity to take a few more pictures to show her family back home.

She smiled as the two bushy tails scampered up one side of a tree, then down the other before heading off to another playground. This was her oasis and she loved it here...every minute of every day.

Tillie placed her phone back into her fanny pack, got to her feet and brushed some earthy residue off her backside. As she stepped back on the path, she heard the footsteps of someone approaching. Not unusual though, as both cyclists and runners alike used this as their favorite trek.

Tillie saw a man moving toward her, rolling a pair of what appeared to be dice between his fingers and palm.

As the middle-aged man drew closer Tillie greeted him with a friendly, "Good morning."

The man looked up, his upper lip twitched, but he didn't utter a sound as he kept walking towards her. As he closed in, Tillie saw blood glistening on his arms and shirt. Her eyes shot to the man's egg shaped face, pitted with ancient acne scars and a three-day growth. She froze, and in that instant the huge man leaped upon her, smashing his massive right fist into her delicate cheekbone. Her head snapped back and she collapsed to the asphalt, wreathing in pain. Without thinking, she reached for her fanny-pack.

Her assailant knelt down and grabbed a hand full of her blond hair and jerked her upwards, his callused fist poised to strike yet another crushing blow. But this time Tillie struck first, plunging her house key deep down into his subclavian artery. Blood spurted out of the jagged wound, painting her Adidas shirt a crimson red.

The big man stumbled backwards but never released his vice like grip on her mangled hair. Tillie struggled to strike again, but the bloody ring of keys slipped from her grip and fell to the ground as she battled to break free. She feared she would die, and there was not a damn thing she could do.

It seemed like a dream...her body being lifted high into the air and launched down the steep bank like a Raggedy Ann doll tossed from a child's crib.

Tillie's head slammed into the ground with excruciating pain. Her last thought was to fight with every fiber of her being. Her twisted body stopped millimeters away from the foaming creek, but watery fingers reached up and grabbed her shapely legs, sucking her into the murky churning water. Her body bobbed a couple of times, disappeared, then popped to the surface again before beginning its frantic race towards the Mississippi.

CHAPTER 2

Tuesday, July 6th

"Spike, come here boy!"

With a couple of slaps to his leg, the black and white Toy Terrier came running and in one bound cleared the three steps to the back porch and came to rest at his master's feet.

"That's my boy. Let's get your collar on before momma has a hissy." Marvin Stocker attached a red leash to the matching neck-strap and together, he and his best friend, headed down the sun-bleached steps.

The bike path began less than two blocks away and Marvin stopped at the entrance until his wife Ethel caught up. Together they walked hand in hand while enjoying one of their peaceful morning strolls along the Duck Creek waterway.

Each morning was a time capsule gathering memories to cherish. On this beautiful July day, they stopped and watched as a Monarch flitted from one purple coneflower to the next. The constant buzz of honeybees gathering pollen also garnered their attention. All of these were part of why they enjoyed these early morning strolls. Yes, the heat and humidity were next to unbearable, but it was worth it.

Their peaceful moment vanished as Spike began yelping and pulling Marvin off the bike path towards the water below.

Spike, spinning like a top, tangled his master's legs with the leash. "Okay, okay, we'll get you some water." Spike was not to be denied as he pulled Marvin ever closer towards the creek bed below.

"Ohhh, God!" Marvin's knees buckled and he landed flat on his butt. He sat there, heart racing, his mouth open, unable to speak and unable to take his eyes off the naked young girl.

Seconds upon mounting seconds passed before he slowly began to crab walk up the incline, trying his best to escape this madness, to put distance between him and the dead girl. But his right hand slipped and blood dripped from his fingers. Not his blood.

"Marvin! Marvin!"

Marvin tried to call out, but no words would form. He couldn't. His tongue froze and his stomach clenched. Yet, he managed to roll over to his knees, and with Spike in tow, worked his way to the top of the embankment.

"Momma, give me your...your phone." His hands shook like a rattler's tail as he frantically punched in 9-1-1.

Chapter 3

Davenport, Iowa's recreational trail

The house phone's ring greeted Davenport's lead homicide detective, Brian Woodford, as he returned from his early morning workout at Gold's Gym.

"Woodford, it's McCreary. We just received a 9-1-1. There's been a murder on Duck Creek's bike path near Harrison and 35th. The Chief just called, said you wouldn't answer your phone. Said to tell you to get your lazy butt out of bed and get to work. His words, not mine."

"Harrison and 35th. Got it. See you in thirty."

Jane always had his back. She was his rock and number one supporter. For him, words of gratitude were hard to share. He'd have to try harder.

Woodford needed to shit, shower, and shave and a couple Ibuprofen would definitely go a long way in helping him overcome a mild hangover.

So much for his long overdue vacation.

Brian popped 800 milligrams of little brown pills and jumped into an icy shower. By the time he'd toweled off the meds had kicked in, and he started to feel like he was ready to take on the world, both the living and the dead.

After dressing in his usual tan slacks, short sleeve blue shirt and power tie, he went into the kitchen where he found his old blood hound hovering over empty food and water bowls. He filled both, grabbed a day-old cherry Danish off the counter and worked his way to the door. His buddy trotted up next to him and nudged his big, loveable head into Brian's leg.

Brian dropped into a squat and gave the dog a friendly shake. "Sorry, buddy, but you'll have to wait until Sylvia gets here for your walk. Dad's got a murder to solve."

Sylvia was a godsend. She kept his house immaculate and she loved his dog. If she wasn't his senior by twenty years he might...nah.

CHAPTER 4

Tuesday, July 6th

The 9-1-1 call came in at 6:20 A.M. The officer on duty, Trent Buckley, dispatched several units and they were on the scene within minutes. Sergeant Carl "Squid" Hawthorne and his rookie partner, Zoe Wilson, were the first responders and parked in one of the many small gravel lots near the bike trail. After crossing a footbridge, they spotted an elderly couple frantically waving in their direction.

Seconds later Hawthorne offered his big meaty paw, but yanked it back after seeing the blood on the old man's hand.

"You okay, sir?" he asked, then turned to the woman. "Ma'am?"

Marvin and his wife shared a look, "No!"

Hawthorne did all he could to settle the poor man down and get a usable statement.

Marvin managed to point his bloody right index finger toward an ancient red oak sixty yards away. "See that bi...big oak? You'll find her body on the other side of the path down by the creek. No hurry though. I'm pretty sure she's dead." His hand still trembled as he stuck it into his baggy pants pocket.

Hawthorne informed the couple a detective would be along shortly to take their statement and directed them to a park bench a few yards away.

The old man nodded a thank you, placed his weathered left hand inside his wife's outstretched arm, and together they moved towards the cast iron bench to wait for the detectives to arrive.

Sergeant Hawthorne worked his way over to the oak and veered to the right side of the path. He peered over the tangled mass of weeds and dead branches. At six-two, he could just make out a patch of yellow cloth and possibly a person's leg. Methodically he worked his way down the incline. Upon reaching the body he checked for vitals, even though it appeared obvious no one could survive such a brutal slaying.

CSI agents George Tandy and Tom Perdan were next on the scene, followed closely by Homicide Detective Jane McCreary and Detectives Harold Steinman and Charlie Owens. McCreary did a quick once over before heading over to interview the elderly couple.

"Shiiiittt!" A single drop of sweat rolled off Perdan's nose and splattered on the victim's left breast. It was becoming a race against time to record and collect evidence before the crime scene became further compromised.

Other than the occasional strands of brunette hair, and massive amounts of blood, no other trace evidence could be found. Nothing. Officers thoroughly marked out, sketched and photographed the area. Blood samples were collected and sent to the lab for identification.

Tandy stopped videotaping when he spotted Homicide Detective Brian Woodford.

"Morning, boss. Watch your step, blood splatter everywhere. By all indications this was the point of attack." Tandy pointed to a pool of blood and flattened weeds.

"Ain't touched the body, been waitin for you," said Perdan.

Their victim lay naked except for a pair of pink panties covering her face. A shoelace from one of her sneakers snaked out from under the yellow shorts. The other shoe lay on top of the tan tank top an arm's distance away. Small beads of dark blood formed lines running down her arms and hips where her clothes had been slashed away. A gash, as clean as a surgical cut, stretched across her neck and teemed with flies. Woodford counted three stab wounds to her lower abdomen. Over kill, he surmised. Even more troubling was that the son of a bitch raped the poor girl with a broken tree branch.

Woodford swallowed some bile inching up his throat and, by chance, looked down the bike path to where Jane was chatting with his witnesses. He hoped they'd be okay, but he couldn't fathom how.

Woodford turned his attention to the young girl lying at his feet. Squatting down, he paused, and then carefully peeled back the pink panties and placed them in an evidence bag along with her other clothes. The girl's vacant emerald green eyes stared back, begging for help, to no avail.

"Bastard!" Woodford said to no one in particular.

CSI Perdan, who was videotaping Woodford's every move, switched back to his DSLR and zoomed in on the neck, face, stab wounds, and pubic area. Damn, he felt like a pervert.

With the help of Squid and Woodford, Tandy and Perdan carefully rolled their victim to her right side. There were no new knife wounds, just deep scratches that zigzagged down the length of her upper torso, the result of being dragged by her feet to her resting place.

Dr. Dan Ball, coroner for the city of Davenport, arrived just as the team finished processing the body.

"Doc..." Woodford paused as he gathered his thoughts. "Our victim appears to be in her early teens, about five-four, and one-ten, give or take. We found no ID and nothing yet from AFIS. Get her back to your lab, do your magic, and let's find the monster responsible for this senseless murder."

CHAPTER 5

Tuesday, July 6th

As Detective Jane McCreary approached the Stockers, Spike gave a low, menacing growl and dug his paws in. But after a stern reproach he dropped to his belly and lay contentedly next to his master's feet, but never once took his eyes off this strange lady.

After introductions, Jane began recording the Stocker's statement. Between the stutters, stammers and Ethel's constant interruptions, McCreary was able to piece together a time-line from Marvin discovering the body, to his 9-1-1 call.

"Mr. Stocker, were you able to identify our murdered victim?"

"No, Ma'am, the panties partially covered her face, and I didn't have the stomach to look."

"That's good. So, did either of you see anyone else or hear anything unusual, perhaps a scream or screeching tires?"

Ethel's hand shot up as if she was still in grade school. "Didn't hear no scream, detective, but when I looked for someone, anyone to help us, I saw this man climb into the back of a dark blue van. He went in butt first, he did. I thought that a bit queer. I called out to him, but he ignored me. Then five minutes later the van pulled out of the lot over there, about the same time I heard the first sirens. Ain't that right, Papa?"

Old man Stocker confirmed his wife's account, but gave her a dirty look for spoiling his story.

After going over everything a second-time, McCreary thanked the Stockers and offered to give them a ride home. They declined, and as they got up to leave, Ethel turned to Marvin.

"I hope it wasn't that cute young girl that we see each morning."

Jane flinched, "Girl...what girl?"

"There's a cute little brunette, about so tall," said Ethel as she put her hand to her hairline. "Says, 'Good morning,' as she races past each day. She reminds me of our granddaughter, Mary Beth. That's our daughter's little girl. We have another granddaughter, name's Becky, she's the oldest and lives with her dad but we hardly ever get to see her because..."

"Now, Ethel, stop airing our dirty laundry. But she's right, detective. We see her most every day. Don't know her name, but sometimes she's got a t-shirt on with an East High raging red bull on the front, if that will help any. Come to think about it, there's usually two or three girls that pass us each morning, but none today. Ain't that right, momma?"

"No, it's the blond that wears the bull's..."

"Momma, it's the brunette and you know it. Why do you always have to disagree?"

"Don't tell me what I know and don't know," quipped Ethel.

For the next ten minutes, it sounded like Abbott and Costello's "Who's on first?" "No, Who's on second." Neither could agree on anything concerning the girls. Finally, Jane shut off her recorder, thanked the Stockers and worked her way over to the parking lot where Ethel saw the dark van.

When she neared the spot, she turned back to the crime scene. It looked to be a sand wedge away for Tiger Woods but at least a five iron for her, assuming she could clear the creek. Who was she kidding? She couldn't get there with a driver.

Turning her attention back to the parking lot she began searching for trace evidence. There were the usual pop tabs, gum wrappers, cigarette butts and...a used condom. These she gathered, bagged and tagged. As she closed her evidence kit a ray of sunlight splashed off something shiny that caught her attention. Blood, a small droplet of blood, then another and another, all glistening, demanded her attention.

Jane cupped her hands, "Woodford, got fresh blood over here!"

McCreary was on one knee flicking bits of gravel away from the blood and studying the ground when Woodford arrived.

"Boss, our witnesses spotted a dark blue van pulling out of this lot about the same time they heard the sirens. Now I'm finding fresh blood. I don't think that's a coincidence, especially this time of morning."

Before Woodford could respond, Ethel's shrill voice reached their ears.

"Detectives...detect...there's a...ringing...here! A phone! It's ringing."

"Jane, go see what she's yapping about. Perdan and I will finish up here."

As McCreary approached the Stockers she could hear no ringing, just Ethel babbling about hearing a phone. Jane put a finger to her lips and shushed the old lady. She could hear plenty of noise, but definitely no ring tones unless they used the sound of insects buzzing about.

Besides being hot and sticky, Jane was frustrated with the Stockers for wasting her time. Just as she decided to call it quits the hint of a ringtone caught her attention.

"See, I told you I heard a phone." Ethel aimed that remark at her husband.

As Jane worked her way toward the ringing, the smell of blood and the cacophony of hundreds if not thousands of buzzing flies battered her senses.

The ringing became progressively louder, then stopped as abruptly as it started. The buzzing of flies replaced the ringtone and McCreary followed the incessant sound until she came to a mass of flies battling for a spot at a bloody dinner table.

"Woodford, you'd better get over here," Jane called to her boss. She was on her hands and knees searching for the phone when Woodford arrived.

The weeds parted, then collapsed back into place as Jane methodically searched the area where she'd heard the phone. Within minutes, the area was being swept by no less than six of Davenport's finest, when a single beep gave away the phone's hiding place.

Wedged between two rocks, the I-phone was nearly impossible to see.

Woodford removed the phone from its hiding place, and as he did so, several strands of blond hair and a trace of blood became visible on one of the stones.

Woodford thumbed the phone on and a message appeared indicating the battery needed to be recharged. He quickly found the cell phone's number just as the image went black.

Using his own phone, he contacted the station and found out the phone belonged to a Tillie Silvermann from Fort Dodge, Iowa. A city 230 miles northwest of Davenport.

So why are you in Davenport, Miss Tillie Silvermann, and where have you gone? thought Woodford.

Tom Perdan, Davenport's resident geek, took the phone and hightailed it back to the station. Who knew what treasures might lay hidden within. But, first he would need to deal with the blood samples.

Their crime scene, now the size of two football fields, was dotted with plain clothes and blue bloods. Their search expanded east along the rushing waters for the elusive Tillie Silvermann.

Woodford made his way back toward the command center while Jane orchestrated the search for Tillie.

His long strides slowed as he used his shirt sleeve to wipe away the sweat and grime from his forehead and upper lip. Silently he cursed the heat, humidity, and the bastard that created the havoc that caused him to be here.

By chance Woodford looked down and saw a coin lying just off the bike path. *Find a penny, pick it up, all day long you'll have good luck.*

He pocketed the shiny new penny and smiled. *Maybe, just maybe, it fell from the perpetrator's pocket?*

Jane caught up and walked with him stride for stride.

Woodford spotted her tagging along. "A penny for your thoughts?"

Jane rubbed the heels of her palms deep into her weary eyes, then slowly pulled them down, stretching the skin, similar to Edward Munch's painting, '*The Scream.*'

"Boss, I have a gut feeling this is going to turn into a double homicide and Tillie Silvermann will be victim number two. At least that's what the evidence points to. My instincts tell me that Tillie was out jogging and probably came across our killer as he was heading to his van. She may have seen something, he kills her, and ditches the body in the creek.

Does any of this sound plausible to you?"

"Another one of your gut feelings?" quipped Woodford. "Before we put a toe tag on Tillie, let's find her body first. Silvermann could have lost that phone days ago and she's having a cold gin and tonic somewhere, oblivious to what took place here today."

As they worked their way back to the first crime scene, the two detectives took turns bouncing ideas off one another, but time and again, their gut instinct told them that before the day ended they'd find Tillie at the bottom of Duck Creek.

Chapter 6

Tuesday, July 6th, Four hours earlier

How could this have happened? He was a trained assassin. Nobody, absolutely nobody, ever got the best of him. Not in Iraq, Afghanistan, or on the streets of Chicago. Then some snot nosed kid, a girl no less, stabs him with a damn key.

Damn you, damn you, damn you!!! I should have killed you, you crazy bitch!

He found one of his precious dice next to the ring of keys, the other die a scant distance away. He picked up all three, pocketed the dice, and chucked the keys as far as he could before taking off to his van. As he crossed the foot bridge to the parking lot he paused and lowered himself to the ground. Blood oozed between his fingers and his brain was struggling to function.

"Keep your head in the game," he muttered. "You've been through worse than this. Keep your head in the game, damn it."

He pulled himself up and pushed off the bridge. Each step became a tussle between his will to live and his fear of death and what the devil had waiting for him. He held no doubt in his mind that Lucifer was saving a special place for him where the fire would burn the hottest and the agony would be far greater than any he'd inflicted on those whose lives he'd taken.

As he reached the van and opened the rear doors he heard an old lady and her husband calling for help. Little did they know that he was the last person they'd want to come to their aid.

Inside the van a box of mismatched clothes yielded an old Cubs t-shirt and a white gym sock. He concocted a makeshift bandage and tied it firmly over the jagged wound, momentarily stopping the flow of blood. Exhaustion was winning the battle of wills and he flopped back against the slatted floorboards.

Thirty seconds, just thirty seconds, and he'd be on his way...

Five minutes later the sound of sirens pierced his blood-deprived brain. Precious seconds ticked by before the cobwebs cleared and he crawled into the front seat. Slowly, he exited the parking lot and took a right on 35th and another right onto Harrison St., just as the first black and white screamed by.

The piercing sound of sirens sent excruciating waves of pain through his eyes and into his brain. A couple blocks later the wail of sirens became muffled, replaced by the thump, thump, thump of his heart echoing in his ears.

At Locust and Harrison, he pulled into the parking lot of the Eye Pavilion, retrieved his cell phone from the drink holder and punched in the number for his buddy, "Tinker".

The phone picked up on the fourth ring. "I's not here now," came the reply. "So, leave your name, number and a message and I'll gets right ba...wait a minute, I thinks I see my car coming up da drive...Nope, dat's not me. You know da drill and I'll get back to you soon as I can." Beeeeeeeeeep.

"Tinker, it's me, as soon as you get this message give me a..."

"That you, Bones?" came the reply.

"Yeah, I'm heading over to your place. Gonna need some stitches."

"Whatcha do this time, get stabbed by one of your whores?"

"Yeah, something like that. Should be there in about thirty," said Bones.

"You got it, buddy. See yah in a quarter and change."

As Bones drove down Harrison Street, he passed Davenport East High School, an elegant structure built around the turn of the 20th century. The old school held many fond memories and he looked forward to East High's 20th high school reunion on the weekend. But if he didn't get this wound taken care of he might not be alive to enjoy the festivities.

He took a right on Fourth Street, a one-way heading west, and stopped for a light at 4th and Marquette where his eyes glazed over and all went dark. Blaring car horns and someone pounding on the passenger side window saved him from the Grim Reaper's strangle hold. He gave a flippant wave to the stranger and put the van in gear.

The rest of the trip was uneventful as he weaved his way to Wisconsin Avenue before pulling into a one-car garage. He pulled the keys from the ignition, slumped down and waited.

***

Seeing the van, Tinker proceeded out to the garage with three fingers of Jack and four cubes, just the way Bones liked it.

"Hey, Bones, get your butt in here. The cubes are starting to melt." Only the ticking of the overheated engine responded to his call.

Bones stood a good three inches taller than Tinker and tipped the scales at 235. Tinker dragged his dying friend out of the garage and into the kitchen where he hooked a foot around a kitchen chair and let Bones slide down into it.

"I gotta close the garage, Bones. You going to be okay?"

"What do you think?" came the weak reply.

Tinker returned to the garage, grabbed the glass of Jack, and allowed the cold brown liquid to trickle down his parched throat. He smacked his lips, hit the remote, and headed back into the house.

Standing over Bones, Tinker undid the makeshift bandage and carefully peeled away the bloodied sock. He gave a soft elongated whistle. "Damn, man. What'd she stick you with?"

It was a rhetorical question that went unanswered.

"Shit, looks like she hit the artery. You lucky to be alive."

Tinker wasn't the saltiest chip in the bag, but his soft hands and nimble fingers could stitch the largest wound and barely leave a scar. This appeared, however, to be much more delicate, and he didn't know if he possessed the skill set to get the job done.

Bones mumbled something about getting started just before the van keys slipped from his limp fingers and clattered to the green and white tiled floor.

"No can do, good buddy. Da thread I got is too heavy for dis suture job. Gotsta go borrow some finer stuff from a friend."

Tinker struggled, but managed to shift the motionless body from the chair to the floor. He then grabbed his car keys off a brass hook by the door, took one last glance over his shoulder and shook his head.

"Bones, what'd you get me into dis time?"

CHAPTER 7

Tuesday, July 6th

Every newspaper and television reporter in the Quad Cities was looking for a tasty tidbit to pass on to their demanding bosses. Woodford hated doing interviews. Questions began flying before he could get within twenty yards.

He coughed twice before beginning. "Ladies and gentlemen, early this morning an unknown person or persons assaulted and killed a young girl whom we believe was out jogging. At this time, we are unable to identify the victim or her assailant. Further information will be passed on as soon as it becomes available. Please, no questions. This ends the interview. Thank you for your patience."

"Hey, Woodford, Quad City Times. One question...was she raped?"

Woodford hated jerks who asked the questions even more than the interviews. He gave the man a universal salute and returned to the crime scene.

McCreary, with the help of Hawthorne and Zoe Wilson, closed down the command center and began loading evidence bags into her car when Woodford cornered her.

"Jane, I'm heading over to Subway. Can I get you anything?"

"A six-inch sub, and Brian, surprise me with *anything* but tuna. And you can throw in a couple of those macadamia cookies."

"Tuna it is, and I'll even splurge for a foot-long."

Jane flashed him a look. "You'd better not."

With a sly grin, he slapped the trunk of Jane's Dodge Charger before heading off to his own vehicle. After a few feet, he turned around, "Still no news on the girl's prints?"

"Nope."

***

Exhaustion seeped into every fiber of Jane's being. Her normal, perfect hair clung to her forehead and her always reliable deodorant wasn't hiding any secrets. The July sun beat down relentlessly and her arms and face were a lobster red, except for the raccoon eyes hidden behind her Foster Grants.

Jane grabbed a bottle of water out of a cooler and splashed some of the cool liquid on her arms and face before guzzling the rest.

Even though no second body had been recovered...yet, Jane believed that most likely another victim would be found, and she would be Tillie Silvermann. Based on the proximity of the phone and the blond hair, she was sure of it. Woodford must have believed the same, because now the search stretched for over a half mile downstream. He would never waste that kind of manpower on a whim. Police were canvassing all homes backing up to the park and, for the third or fourth time, searched all the grounds surrounding the area where their murdered victim was found. Still nothing.

Jane chose one of the big shady oaks and plopped down with her back against the trunk. The crime scene made no sense. A young girl was grabbed from behind while jogging, had her neck sliced from ear to ear, and then was dragged down an embankment, stripped of her clothes, stabbed, and raped with a branch. Still, no evidence was recovered. The guy must be a pro. But why here? Why her? Jane's head spun.

And then, no more than a hundred yards away, they found another blood spill and a phone belonging to a Tillie Silvermann, but no body. Where was Tillie? Could she have been taken hostage, or was she hidden under the churning waters of Duck Creek? Or maybe she escaped and was in hiding. Maybe, maybe, maybe...

Zoe Wilson, one of the first police officers on the scene, called out. "Detective McCreary, I've got something! Detective McCreary!"

Jane met up with Zoe, who'd been searching the ball field south of the bike path and spotted a shiny object in the grass.

"When I spotted these keys, I thought it was a crushed beer can, but then realized it was a key ring coated with blood." She held it out with a gloved hand for Jane to see.

Jane carefully noted the three keys: one for a Toyota and the other two resembling typical house keys. The longer of the two had pieces of what appeared to be flesh lodged between the teeth. Also, attached to the ring was a Mississippi Valley Blood Donor's card. No name, but the donor was A negative.

Jane fished her phone from her front pocket and thumbed in five. On the third ring, Woodford answered. She gave him an abbreviated version of what Zoe found.

"Be right there," he said.

***

Woodford tossed the rest of his lunch into his desk drawer and bolted for his car.

His siren's scream pierced the silence along Duck Creek and ended with the sound of tires crunching on gravel. Jane met him there with the keys dangling from her pen.

"Boss, I've got what looks to be skin, blood, and a white thread on one of the keys."

Woodford removed gloves and an evidence bag from his back pocket. Slipping on the gloves, he took the keys and studied them before turning his attention to the donor card. Careful not to smudge any prints, he detached the card and placed it into an evidence bag.

"Jane, I want you to hustle over to the blood center and get a name. Contact me as soon as you find out who the donor is. Afterwards, get the card to the lab and see if there are any prints or DNA our killer may have left behind. I'll do the same with the keys. Cross your fingers.

"By the way, your lunch is in the fridge. But, I ate the cookies."

After all she does for the team, he just didn't have the heart to tell her the sub was tuna.

CHAPTER 8

Tuesday, July 6th

Woodford squirmed in his seat as he drove back to the station. This was their first real lead and he couldn't wait to get the keys back to the lab and hear what McCreary discovered. If all went well, he might still salvage a few days of vacation. Hell, if they caught their killer, Chief Angel might even tack on a few days of paid leave.

The offices were quietly busy as he worked his way down to the lab where he dropped off the keys. Crossing the hall to Perdan's cubical, he retrieved Tillie's phone and proceeded to his office on the second floor. He rummaged through a junk drawer until he found a charger and plugged in Tillie's phone. First priority, the directory.

Where's Jane? The thought soon vanished as he turned his attention back to the contact list. One by one he made his calls. His exchange was the same for everyone.

He gave his name without title, and told them he'd found this phone and wondered if anyone knew how he could get in touch with Tillie Silvermann. No sense in getting them riled up over what possibly might be nothing at all. Every contact had a 515-prefix attached to the number and their owners all lived in Fort Dodge, Iowa, home of the St. Edmond Gaels. After talking to an aunt, he discovered Tillie came to Davenport to train for the upcoming Bix 7 road race. No one had talked to Tillie for days, if not weeks.

He checked her e-mails, texts, Facebook, and downloads. Nothing came to light of what might have happened to the mysterious Miss Silvermann. Unable to crack the password to her voicemail, he turned to her photographic files. There were thirteen folders with thousands of images. All the folders were dated, but none covering the last forty-eight hours. He chose to ignore those, instead looked at the individual photos dated Tuesday, July 6th. He carefully studied each image.

Ground hogs and squirrels. Image after spectacular image showed Tillie as a budding photographer. The two photographs of squirrels were exceptionally artistic and proved, at least in Brian's opinion, that Tillie possessed a great eye for her craft.

The last two images caught and held Woodford's undivided attention. Far off in the distance a human figure could be seen...definitely a man. Could it be she'd captured their suspect? He couldn't wait to get the phone back to the lab and see, if anything, what Agent Perdan might unveil.

He checked his watch. Jane left for the blood center well over an hour ago. *Watch pots never boil,* he told himself. His adrenalin was flowing like Niagara Falls and be it nerves or a tick, he unwittingly checked his watch for the umpteenth time.

His desk phone rang, but it wasn't Jane.

Brian recognized the voice as Tom Perdan. "Boss, based on two sets of prints, the keys definitely belong to Tillie. We also dug into her history and discovered she's 22 and blond. We suspect it's the same color as the wisp of hair found on the rock." He continued, "Tandy and I were able to extract blood and skin from one of the keys and sent samples to Marine Corps in Quantico, Virginia for DNA testing. It's going to take weeks, so be patient."

"Great job, guys! You two deserve a pat on the back and a fine howdy-do. As a fitting reward, here's something you can stick your teeth into. I just went over the images from Tillie's phone. There are a few surprises you need to see. I'm not going to spoil the moment, but you need to hustle up here. This just became your number one priority."

"Got it, boss. I'm practically knocking on your door."

Brian pushed his chair away from his desk and stretched to his full capacity. His mind began to wander, *Would they really be able to identify their killer? Could they be that lucky?* He pushed that thought from his mind and turned his thoughts to Tillie. *No body, no murder. Not yet anyway.*

***

Jane dropped the donor's card off at the lab before heading up to speak with Woodford.

"Where've you been, bright eyes?"

"Don't ask. I got called to break up a fight between two idiots over a minor fender-bender. Thanks to Seri, I located the Regional Blood Center and talked to the head of staff.

"She informed me the card belongs to Tillie Silvermann as we suspected. She's 22, blond, and five-six."

Jane paused, took a deep breath and a bite of her half-eaten tuna sub. It was all she'd eaten, and even though she didn't care much for the day's catch, it all tasted really good at the moment, especially the cup of Joe.

Brian didn't want to spoil Jane's enthusiasm, so deferred in spilling the beans that Perdan already passed on much of the information Jane just shared.

***

The warrant to search Tillie's apartment arrived and the two detectives headed over in hopes of finding their missing girl alive.

Ten metallic mailboxes were in the foyer just to the right as they entered. The second box from the bottom indicated a T. Silvermann lived on the ground floor, apartment three. The sound of Woodford's knock resonated down the hallway causing more than one head to poke out from behind closed doors.

Woodford knocked a second time, a little louder and longer. Identical result.

An elderly lady, with tin cans rolled into her purple hair, rapped her cane against the wall to gain attention.

"Hey, mister, ain't seen Tillie all day, but I sure heard her leave early this morning, just like every morning."

"Thanks, Hilda!" called the manager as he worked his way through a bundle of keys. Woodford nudged the manager aside and picked the door's lock within seconds. The two detectives entered, guns drawn.

It was a small efficiency apartment, one bedroom, bath and kitchen. Something a single person might typically have. There were no pictures on the wall and no Tillie, just a few personal items in the bath and bedroom and plenty of health food in the fridge. Most of Tillie's belongings were still in boxes stacked haphazardly in the bedroom closet. There were no signs of a live-in boyfriend or roommate. The only thing out of place appeared to be a teddy on an unmade bed.

Jane stepped outside in hopes of finding a Toyota. A red Celica convertible, in cherry condition, was parked a couple of doors down.

The block's busybody stopped pruning his rose bushes long enough to eyeball McCreary. "That Toyota belongs to the cute little blond whose apartment complex you just came out of."

"I'm looking for Miss Silvermann, the cute little blond. Have you seen her today?" asked Jane.

"No, usually she's up at the crack of dawn and off on her daily run. Something happen to her?"

"Not sure. May have been a witness to a crime this morning. I need to speak with her. If you see her, give the station a call," and handed him her business card.

He took the card, tucked it into the top pocket of his bibs, and whistled a little tune as he turned back to his precious roses.

Jane found Tillie's car unlocked, but that was all she found.

As she finished up her initial inspection, Woodford exited the apartment complex and motioned for her to get in the car. He just received a 10-19 call to return to the station. A frantic and distraught woman was demanding to see their Jane Doe.

CHAPTER 9

Tuesday, July 6th

Amy Porter ricocheted like a pinball from one chair to the next, then out the door and back. Frustration peaked as she waited for Detective Woodford. Her daughter was missing and she wanted answers. Not knowing was tearing her apart.

"Where's your damn detective!" she screamed. Out the door she flew, straight into Woodford, nearly bowling him over. Amy collapsed to the floor, sobbing with one breath, and apologizing with the next. She took a Kleenex from her handbag, blew her nose and wiped the tears and mascara from her eyes. As she reached for Woodford's outstretched hand their eyes met, and Woodford knew. He'd seen those same eyes that morning when he removed the panties from the young runner's face.

Amy stood and gazed into Woodford's eyes...

"Brian, Brian Woodford? Remember me? Amy Bergthold. Well, Amy Porter now."

How could he forget? He and Amy were "a thing" all through high school, long before his family moved to Florida seeking employment. Years went by, both married, and their dreams of the perfect life soon faded to distant memories.

An awkward silence fell between them. His giddiness at seeing his long-lost soul-mate vanished as he came to grips with the moment.

Brian's poker face gave away the hollowness he felt in his stomach. Amy was no fool. She recognized the pain in Woodford's eyes and knew instantly that she'd never see her daughter alive again.

"Noooooooooooooo!" The scream echoed throughout the halls and into every cubicle. Heads and eyes raised, then quickly averted.

This time the eyes of the mother and detective met and held, hers pleading that he was wrong. His, begging for forgiveness for being the bearer of tragic news.

Amy dug through her purse and found a wallet photo of her daughter and handed it to Detective Woodford.

The photo showed a girl with shorter and redder hair than the murder victim. The genuine smile belonged to someone who loved life. Two deep dimples pierced her rosy cheeks. Her eyes were carbon copies of her mother's, emerald green with little creases at the corners. Their murder victim that morning was no longer a Jane Doe, but rather Liz "Lizzie" Porter.

Seventeen, honor student, artist and musician who loved school, her teachers and friends. Above all else she lived and breathed for track, her true passion and love.

At 5:30 A.M Lizzie's eyes would pop open; no alarm was ever needed. Every morning she jogged out the door before six and ran five miles, hot or cold, rain or snow. This morning was no different.

The interview in Woodford's office ended quickly.

Lizzie's mom heard about the murder from a co-worker at lunch. At the end of her shift she'd raced home to find three voice mails. One from Lizzie's boss at Younkers asking why she failed to show for work. Numbers two and three were from a Becky Ahlstrom, a sales clerk and Lizzie's friend. "Liz, if you're with that creep Billy, text and tell me all about it." Amy didn't know this Billy, nor could she think of anyone who would want to kill her precious daughter.

Amy tried to stand but slumped back into her chair. Her chin dropped to her chest where it bobbed with every heart-wrenching beat.

Time ticked by as Amy Porter struggled to gain composure. Finally, in a voice soft and weak, she asked if she could see her daughter.

Woodford helped her to her feet and handed the photograph back. Amy softly kissed the image and lovingly placed it back in her purse. McCreary took a hand and Woodford an arm as they guided Amy Porter out to the parking lot.

The ride to the morgue was as silent as death itself.

Chapter 10

Tuesday, July 6th

The basement level of Genesis East Hospital held Davenport's City Morgue. Brian parked in the east lot, and with Jane's help, led Amy inside where they met the city's coroner, Dr. Dan Ball.

After explaining the procedures of identification, Ball retreated to the inner-morgue where he retrieved the gray steel gurney holding the remains of Liz Porter. The wheels squeaked and squawked as Doc Ball rolled the gurney toward the viewing window. Once in place, he took the top two corners of the sheet and carefully folded it back, exposing the angelic face of Liz Porter, but not the hideous scar.

Amy's eyes pleaded with Woodford, begging him to let her spend time with her little girl, but the autopsy needed to be completed. With much misgiving, Amy rested her forehead against the cold hard glass, her trembling hands pressed against the unforgiving window.

Detectives Woodford and McCreary stepped down the hall to the commissary to give Amy time alone with her daughter. Coroner Ball tucked the sheet a little tighter around Lizzie's shoulders, then stepped into his inner sanctum, leaving the grieving mother alone.

***

Silence enveloped the viewing room. Amy watched the others leave, then turned and looked lovingly at her precious daughter. A single tear appeared that she blinked away, but another took its place.

She closed her eyes. Warmth, like an early morning sun, enveloped her. Her body melted through the plate glass window and a smile creased her face as she reached out for her adorable daughter.

A single finger of her right hand made little ringlets in Lizzie's hair. Her lips softly caressed Lizzie's forehead and cheeks.

Her arms wrapped around her daughter and embraced her and she was hugged back. Words of love passed between mother and daughter. Loving words that had never been spoken before were spoken now. Promises were made to love each other forever and a day, and a day and a day...

Mother pulled away from daughter and their eyes met, mirrored eyes, both flowing with tears, both green as the Emerald Iles. Fingers touched, kisses were blown and whispers of goodbye were shared.

Once again, the cold of the morgue crept into her bones and Amy found herself alone. She opened her eyes and saw Woodford and McCreary waiting for her.

***

Woodford's heart ached. He really was a softy. Not that he'd ever let his team know.

"I'm sorry we couldn't let you be with your daughter," he said.

Amy gave an unknowing smile, "That's okay. We said our goodbyes."

Since Amy Porter seemed to be in no condition to drive, Woodford dropped McCreary at the station and then drove Amy home.

Woodford rounded the last corner and pulled into the circular drive. A stately woman, her silver hair tied in a bun, stood in the open door. A cloak of anguish masked her face.

A moment of silent heartache was shared before Woodford opened the car door for Amy and accompanied her to the front porch landing where they were met by the elderly woman.

"Mr. Woodford, this is my mother, Nana Bergthold. She lives with Liz and me, I mean..."

Woodford accepted an invitation to come in for a cup of tea. He kept his questions to a bare minimum. There would be time for that in the morning. They agreed to meet the next day around 10:00, give or take, and Woodford bid his farewell.

Brian's heart ached for this poor woman. As he walked back to his car he made a solemn promise to himself that nothing, absolutely nothing, would stop him from finding Liz's killer. Not now, not ever.

CHAPTER 11

Tuesday, July 6th

It was 6:25 P.M by the time Woodford arrived home from the Porter's. Clouds rolled in and claps of thunder were heard coming from the west. The temperature dropped to a balmy eighty-five.

The game, Dog vs. Man, began. Brian's goal: remove food and a drink from the fridge and eat one bite before the dog was by his side. Stakes...winner takes all.

Asleep in the spare bedroom waited his opponent, "Barker." The old hound's name honored the TV star and animal activist Bob Barker.

Brian and his dog played this game most every night, a game he'd never won. Tonight would be different. He'd parked his car down the street so there'd be no crunching of gravel. He removed his penny loafers at the door and silently placed them on the floor.

His muscles ached as he inched toward the fridge door and his left-over tuna casserole. He'd removed the fridge bulb the night before just in case that was the bug-a-boo giving him away.

He was Lead Detective. He was the man. The dog stood no chance.

Brian eased the refrigerator door open. Nothing rattled, not a sound. The tuna casserole was all his, and now for a cold Bud Light. He lifted the icy cold bottle from the rack. He stole a peek, no dog. Should he rip off the foil and spoon out a mouthful or play fair? Play fair, he decided. He stepped back to close the door and a yelp came from the dog standing behind him the whole time. Dog 38. Detective 0.

He put his makeshift meal back in the fridge and grabbed the leash.

As he left his house a light mist started to fall which felt good, but hardly the remedy he needed for his aching bones. Fifteen minutes later he returned to the house.

"Dang it!" He'd forgotten to pick up dog food. It killed him, but he took the leftover tuna and noodles and scraped it into the dog's dish. He checked the fridge for any other leftovers. Finding none, he settled for a Swiss cheese, bologna and mustard sandwich on rye.

Before the second piece of bread topped his makeshift meal, Barker was by his side begging for more. Woodford took his sandwich and cold beer into the den, plopped down in his favorite chair and turned to channel 6 to watch Wheel of Fortune. His ever-hopeful hound sat next to him, his big brown eyes staring up, begging for anything that might fall his way.

"S * N N I N G - S * R * I N G - * N * - S * I * * I N G

"Sunning, surfing and swimming," called out Woodford.

Woodford ate all but one bite of his sandwich and tossed the last morsel into the air. Not so much as a crumb hit the floor. He just wished his beloved Cubs were as accurate at catching line drives. After licking the last of the Gray Poupon from his lips, the big hound looked up at his master with a sigh of appreciation.

At long last, Woodford stripped down and basked in the shower he'd longed to have.

Every muscle in his body ached and he was going to soak forever. He had just settled in, steaming water pounding down on his face and shoulders, when someone rapped on the bathroom door.

"Woodford, I've been trying to reach you. Don't you ever answer your phone?" called out Detective McCreary.

She wasn't angry, perturbed, maybe.

Brian dried off, wrapped himself in a fluffy cotton towel and shuffled into the kitchen where he smelled coffee brewing.

Jane looked up from her steaming cup. "Go get dressed. Have I got a story for you!"

Upon his return, he found Jane sitting in his leather recliner with his dog's head in her lap.

"Barker, get over here, you traitor." The old dog slowly got up and ambled over to Woodford who grabbed him by the ears and gave his head a friendly shake.

"So, what's so earth shattering that you interrupted my shower?"

"Brian, this is so cool. This kid...name's..." she pulled out her notes, "Dusty Anders, is a photography student at Scott Community College. He was working on an assignment when he came across a blond mannequin snagged on a tree stump. He thought it would look cool in his dorm room. So, he slid down the embankment and grabbed it by the hair. Imagine the shock when the manikin screamed. He lost his footing and tumbled into Duck Creek, losing his phone and camera along the way. Fighting the current, he managed to free the girl and the two-floated down stream until he found an area where he struggled to haul her ashore. Then he carried her a couple of blocks back to his truck and took her to the hospital. Yup, it was Tillie!"

"Bullshit...really? Is she ok?"

"Hardly. Tillie remained stuck on that log for hours. She's lucky to be alive. The funny thing is, she's been at Genesis since late this afternoon."

Jane continued, "I got in touch with her parents and they're on their way from Fort Dodge. After the call, I hoofed it over to Genesis where I met the Anders kid and talked to your buddy Dr. Oberhaus. He..."

Before Jane could finish, Woodford grabbed his keys and ran out the door. Over his shoulder he yelled, "Lock up! You're coming with me!"

Woodford was furious that no one bothered to contact him, right up until..."Damn!" He didn't even have to look. He remembered shutting off his phone when he interviewed Amy Porter and he never turned it back on. *Dumb, dumb, dumb,* but pride wouldn't allow him to admit it.

For the rest of the trip, silence prevailed.

"I posted a guard," said Jane, "in case our murderer wants another crack at Tillie." It was enough to break the awkwardness as they ascended to the third floor.

Officer Tommy Olson, snacking on a Twinkie when they arrived, cleared his lips of white goo before informing them, "Doc's in."

Tillie lay there, pale as the sheets that were tucked under her chin.

Card player, left fielder, beer drinker and close friend, Dr. Oberhaus turned his head to look at his buddy Woodford. "Wondered when you'd get here. Nurse, would you take over for me?" Oberhaus grabbed Woodford by the elbow. "Let's step into the hall."

Oberhaus barely spoke above a whisper. "Brian, Tillie's gone through hell and back. I can't imagine being bashed about by raging water for hours, wondering if you'd live or die. Her body took a beating. She has a hairline fracture of her right mandible and a broken nose. A knot on the frontal bone is the size of a walnut from when she smacked her head against a rock. I'm confident these injuries should all heal quickly, but her brain? That's another matter."

Oberhaus led Woodford and McCreary another ten feet down the hall. "Brian, Tillie suffered a severe concussion. She's in and out of consciousness and remembers nothing of the attack. We should know more within the next twenty-four to forty-eight hours, but these things...well, we just don't know. Keep your fingers crossed.

"Why don't you two pack it in for the night? You both look like road kill," said Oberhaus with a grin.

***

The drive back to Woodford's was quiet and subdued. Jane told about chasing down Becky Ahlstrom while she worked a double shift at Younkers.

"The second I mentioned Billy's name, Becky clammed up tighter than a...a clam. Becky did pass on another name, Sue Hatfield, supposedly Liz's best friend. I was ready to pursue that lead when the call came in that they'd found Tillie."

Jane finished up just as they reached the turn-off to Woodford's bungalow. Jane wanted nothing more than to soak in a hot tub and sip a glass of wine, so she declined the offer of a cold beer and animal crackers.

The light rain earlier now turned into a full-fledged gutter buster as lightning boogied across the sinister skies. As McCreary sat behind the wheel of her car, she said a prayer of thanks for Dusty Anders and another that Tillie would make a full recovery.

CHAPTER 12

Wednesday, July 7th

Sleep usually came easily for Woodford, but not on this night. Images of Liz Porter's mutilated body, intertwined with those of her grieving mother, peppered his restless night. Then a blond mannequin screamed at him to do something, and the buzzing of flies and the metallic smell of blood all made for a fitful night's sleep.

Tick...Tock...Tick...Tock.

The night dragged on.

A shot rang out and he bolted upright. Nothing more than the daily rag slapping against the front stoop.

Had he slept? He didn't think so. His nerves were frazzled and his eyelids refused his mental commands. Worse yet, he solved nothing during the night, not one meaningful thought, not a clue or inkling. He flung his feet off the bed and went to retrieve his paper.

After his first cup of coffee and a couple of waffles that weren't microwaved thoroughly, he settled in to read the daily news.

The Quad City Times accurately reported Liz's murder, except for a couple of misspellings. Thankfully they withheld the victim's name until relatives could be notified. However, he was enraged that someone from his office, without authorization and remaining anonymous, gave out vital information that Woodford wanted kept from the public. In particular, the rape and three stab wounds.

Another small article mentioned a girl nearly drowning and that was exactly how he wanted it played. No names, no clues. He feared for Tillie's life, especially if her attacker realized a potential witness remained alive.

He finished the article, flipped the page, and saw himself in all his glory, giving the finger to the Quad City Times reporter. His ass was grass and the mayor would do the mowing. The day couldn't get any worse, and it was only 7:30.

After his daily workout at Gold's gym and a leisurely walk with Barker, he was ready to attack whatever came his way. He checked his watch: 9:05 and time to give Amy Porter a call. He found her number, entered it into his cell, and programmed it to speed dial #9.

Before the call even connected he pressed end. If Mrs. Porter's night mirrored anything close to what he went through, she could use another hour of sleep. He'd call later.

Brian did a little two-step to get around the dew worms that littered the sidewalk after the storm the night before. He hated to see all that bait going to waste, but murder waits for no one. Not even slimy ten-inch crawlers.

The second floor buzzed with activity as he stepped out of the elevator. One-fingered greetings were offered at every turn as he made his way to his office. As he passed McCreary's cubicle, she smiled at him as was her nature and tossed him the morning's hot sheet.

"Another murder," she began. "This time in Rock Island."

Rock Island, a city of 45,000, lay across the Mississippi River from Davenport. Brian skimmed the paperwork. This killing had all the signs of another gang fight gone wrong. He recognized the name of the deceased, a Jesse Rodriquez, aka, 'Peyote.' Rodriquez had a reputation as a known banger and a nasty, ill-tempered man. Word on the street was he'd raped and killed a rival's bitch, so it was no surprise he ended up at the city morgue.

"I've always said, too much alcohol, heavy doses of drugs, plus this crazy summer heat, makes for a deadly cocktail."

Jane agreed.

"As long as it stays on the east side of the river I'll be a happy man." Woodford continued to skim the morning's hot sheet. "Bar fights, abused wives, two separate robberies at local Kwik Shops, hookers and a drug bust..." He looked at Jane. "Sounds like another day in paradise."

"Keep reading," Jane told him. "There's another name you might be interested in, the one on the pink sticky note. Woodford, the

Hale woman says she knows you. Give her a call."

He turned the name over in his mind but it didn't sound familiar. "Mary Hale," he repeated. Still, it didn't ring a bell.

According to Jane, Mary Hale reported that a middle-aged man kept stalking her daughter, April. April spotted the man following her home from school and again while at the market. He picked up the phone and dialed the number. Voice mail answered and he left a message to call him back.

There were several yellow sticky notes attached to his computer screen. One in particular caught his eye. The coroner wanted to see him ASAP.

***

Ball was going over notes when Woodford arrived at the morgue. Brian pushed a couple of periodicals aside and plopped down on the mahogany desk.

Ball got straight to the point. "Brian, Liz Porter wasn't raped in the truest sense of the word. No sign of sperm or bodily fluids nor any residue from a condom. The stick penetrated the vagina post mortem, just like the stab wounds. Also, she was not pregnant, nor do I believe she was sexually active. It sickens me that some animal would deliberately brutalize this young lady in such a hideous fashion."

"Dan, do you believe this slaying was personal, or a spur of the moment act of self-indulgence?"

"Brian, the fact that he covered her face with the panties almost proves a personal connection. In my professional opinion, this vile act can be attributed to someone who knew her. I'd bet my Iowa season tickets that our suspect is related to our victim or a hired assassin. Either way, he's sick and needs to be removed from the face of the earth."

Brian listened intently, making several mental notes.

Ball interlocked his fingers over his head and closed his eyes. He took several seconds before continuing.

"Brian, let's assume, I know we're not supposed to assume, so let's presume that Liz was out jogging. Our assailant chases her down, grabs onto her hair with his left hand, causing her head to jerk backwards so violently that it snaps two of her vertebra. And, in one swift and precise motion, slashes Lizzie's neck from ear to ear. Brian, this powerful move nearly severed the spinal cord. Death would have been instantaneous. This man knew exactly what he was doing and executed it to perfection."

Another piece of information Brian stored into his photo-like memory bank.

Ball continued, "Liz was five-four and a hundred and twelve pounds. To achieve the leverage to make the cut that killed Liz, your assailant had to be at least six-two, possibly six-four. This was no mama's boy. We also know from the angle of the cut that he was right handed," Ball continued.

"Our killer manages to attack a trained athlete from behind while she's running, no less. He jerks her head back and slices her throat, drags her down the ravine, takes the time to cut off her clothes, puts her underwear over her head and stabs her three times. Oh, yeah, and then savagely rapes her with a branch. I get why he might want to strip her down, but why take the time to take off her shoes?

"Then, a hundred yards farther down the bike path, we find a second blood spill of considerable amount. We know Tillie didn't lose all that blood because she's A negative, and it couldn't have come from Liz, because that murder happened over a hundred yards away. DNA will explain a lot, but that's days, if not weeks, away. So, if it's not Tillie's or Liz's blood, then it's our killer's. And yet, after losing two to three pints of blood, our killer manages to make it to his van and drive away. So why didn't he kill Tillie? Why did he throw her in the creek instead of slicing and dicing her like he did Liz? And the old couple never heard a thing! Come on, Woodford, say something. You're the man, at least that's what you keep telling me."

Brain nodded, "You're right. It was a senseless, savage attack on a helpless victim. Now, here's what I've got. The Stocker's statement, and I called to confirm it, says they saw a man crawl into the back of a van butt first. But he didn't drive off for at least five minutes. So, I wonder. Did he pass out from loss of blood, catch a couple of ZZZ's, or does he get his rocks off as a reward? My guess is he passed out and the sounds of the sirens brought him to his senses."

Brian continued, "Now, if you really want spooky, at 6:45 A.M we received a 9-1-1 claiming there's a dead body in a blue van at Marquette and 4th. But then the guy hangs up. So, we trace the call and the dude says he banged several times on the passenger side window and poof, the driver sits up and takes off. That's our guy, right? Don't know. Does our caller get a plate? Hell, no! We have a car at the scene within five. No van, no dead body, and no cameras. The van does a Houdini. We're still canvasing the area for cameras and possible witnesses, but so far, zilch.

"We found no trace evidence on Liz, and if there was trace on Tillie, it washed away the second she did a header into the water. Our whacko is probably dead somewhere in a frickin' garage and we won't find his body for a month of Sundays. I don't mind telling you, but this case bites the big one. However, I do have one very titillating bit of news. We have a picture of our killer."

"Bullshit, really?"

"Ok, perhaps that's a bit over the top. Still, I checked Tillie's phone and found pics taken the morning of the killing. In one of her pictures you can see the killer surfacing from the creek bed. The next image shows him walking down the path. There was only one person, so we know he was a lone killer. Good, right? There's only one problem. We have no facial recognition. Poor image quality because the figure was too far away. However, some good news. A sign next to him allows us to calculate his height. And like you estimated, he's 6'3", so things are coming together. The lab is still trying to enhance the images, so keep your fingers crossed."

Woodford checked his watch for the umpteenth time before calling it quits. He previously scheduled his interview with Amy Porter to begin at 10:00. At 9:40 Woodford finally placed the call to Amy. Nana answered and thanked him when Brian suggested a later meeting time.

He had plenty of time, so made his way across town to his favorite Starbucks for coffee and a donut.

CHAPTER 13

Wednesday, July 7th

Detective Jane McCreary exited the elevator at Genesis East and found Duty Officer Allison Tooney rubbing the eraser end of a yellow #2 pencil deep into her scalp. As if that would help her with the Quad City Times crossword puzzle.

Spotting McCreary, she asked, "Jane, what's a six-letter word for door topper?"

"Did you try lintel?"

"Duh, I suck at these things." Tooney erased a couple of squares and inserted the word lintel before dropping the folded paper and taking off for a much-needed potty break.

Jane eased the door open just a crack and peeked in to find Tillie sound asleep.

Jane took the seat vacated by Tooney and picked up the discarded pencil and crossword. By the time Tooney returned Jane finished both the crossword and the daily Sudoku.

"So, Tooney, what's the doc got to say about our hero?"

"Better, much better, but she's still not out of the woods. Any news on the case?" asked Tooney.

"Woodford's talking to Amy Porter as we speak. Hopefully something will come of that. Otherwise, nothing that makes any sense. Keep a close eye on our girl and..." Jane waved the paper, "sorry about finishing your puzzle."

Next on her to-do list was a meet and greet at Emeis Golf Course with Sue Hatfield. Perhaps she'd be more forthcoming than Lizzie's other, so-called friend.

CHAPTER 14

Wednesday, July 7th

The car's digital clock read 10:52 A.M as Woodford arrived at the Porter's residence. Brian loved elegant old homes and this 19th century English Tudor was to die for. The wrap around porch was smothered in potted plants, sporting a variety of flowers of every color and hue. *Magnificent.* Floral motif stained glass lined the portico. The whole package was a work of art that delighted his senses.

He pressed the doorbell. A soft tune he didn't recognize echoed from inside the home. *Oh, but to dream.*

The dream ended with a sigh as Nana greeted Woodford and graciously invited him inside.

"Good morning, Detective. Amy is waiting for you in the den. And be kind, she spent a dreadful night crying and pacing the floor," said Nana.

The den, to the right of the mammoth entry way, overflowed with antiques, almost to the point of gaudiness. The room displayed a musical theme: a player piano stood in one corner, violins, clarinets, and a brass trumpet hung from the ornate papered walls. At least three crank Edison phonographs and a golden harp were scattered amongst the 19th century furnishings. But little of that mattered as Brian looked down upon Amy Porter.

Somehow, she'd aged ten years overnight. Her eyes were empty shells, the pearls stolen.

Amy patted the couch, a subtle invitation for him to join her.

Brian sat and took the fragile, quivering hand she offered. He avoided eye contact at first, preferring to comment on the beautiful Tiffany chandelier.

Amy would have none of it.

"Please, Detective, we must talk. What may I call you?"

The raspberry tea Nana placed before him tasted a bit tart, but refreshing with just a hint of mint. The wafer cookie he left untouched. Brian adjusted his tie and took a deep breath and began.

"Because of our past history, you may call me Brian or Detective Woodford, whichever feels more appropriate."

Brian took another sip of the tea and a snippet of the cookie. The raucous ticking of a grandfather clock and a single chime, too loud for the somber moment, interrupted his chain of thought, but it gave him a moment to gather his wits before beginning the interview.

"Amy, tell me about Lizzie, what was she like?"

Tick...Tock...Tick...Tock

Amy raised her head and Woodford saw a hint of a twinkle in her eyes.

"She was an angel, the perfect child. Shame on me, Detective, I suppose all mothers say the same thing. But really, she was the perfect child. I never needed to scold or correct her. She earned straight A's and last year was president of her class. And, oh, could she run...like the wind. Oh, how I'm going on. Please forgive my pride."

"That's okay. Please continue."

The quiet conversation returned to track and Lizzie's love of running. "Liz was so looking forward to her senior track season. Running meant everything to her," said Amy.

"Did Liz always run so early in the morning, or was yesterday out of the ordinary?" asked Woodford.

"During the school year, her cross-country coach would have them up early and running a minimum of two miles before class every day. He said it was good for the body and the mind. She just got used to it, I guess. So, like clockwork, she's up and out the door before I even shower."

"Do you know the coach's name?"

"Clint Ashford's the varsity coach. He'd do anything to help the girls succeed and the team adores him. He has an assistant, but his name eludes me. Sorry."

Woodford scratched a quick note: talk to Coach Ashford. Girls might like him too much?

"Amy, is there a Mr. Porter?"

Amy looked at Nana and said nothing. Nana filled the awkward gap. "What Amy won't tell you, Mr. Woodford, is that James, Lizzie's dad, is a worthless drunk and womanizer. Amy kicked him out of the house six months ago for slapping Liz when she came home ten minutes late for dinner. That's when I moved in to help out while my girls were getting used to being alone."

"Amy, excuse me for asking, but are you still married?"

"We are," said Amy. "Only because James won't sign the divorce papers. He swears Liz isn't his so he'll be damned if he'll pay child support."

"This could be important, so I must ask. Is James the father?"

Looking up, Amy turned to her mother and then back to Brian.

"I believe so, at least that's the lie I've been telling myself all these years. Liz came ten months after James left for Iraq. I'd divorced my first husband a couple years before. The second James was deployed, Ricky, that's my first husband, popped back into my life. One night things went a little too far." She stopped, stole a glance at her mother, and mouthed the words, "I'm sorry." She continued, "There's no excuse for what I did, detective. I was lonely and he was there for me. That wasn't like me. It just...happened."

"Does James know that he may not be the father?"

"NO! Well...he might have speculated about it later, but he never questioned me when I called and told him we were the parents of a new baby girl. Once his tour finished and he came home, you'd think he was the only man who'd ever fathered a new baby.

"But something happened. Perhaps he became suspicious, did a DNA test, or perhaps Lizzie looked more like Ricky. I don't really know. But, these last two years, you'd have thought he'd become possessed by the devil. His attitude towards Liz went from pampering to hostile. Once I kicked him out he demanded a paternity test be done. But I refused. I was afraid that if Liz turned out to be Ricky's he'd probably kill me and Ricky, too."

"What's Ricky's last name?"

"Porter. Yeah, you'd think after one Porter I would have had enough sense not to marry another one. James is Ricky's cousin."

Woodford became increasingly uncomfortable. This was the lady he once wanted to marry. He crisscrossed his legs several times before taking another sip of tea. What he wouldn't do for a cold beer right now.

Finally, "Do you know what branch of service James served in?"

"I believe he was in Special Forces, but he never talked about it much. He always told me, '*If I tell you what I do, I'd have to kill you.*' I believed him." Amy squirmed in her seat, took a sip of her favorite tea and waited to be judged by Brian.

"Did he ever strike you?"

"No, it was more verbal abuse than physical. A few times he'd grab and shake me, but he never hit me. That's why I was so shocked when he slapped Liz."

"I need to get in touch with James. Do you know where he lives now?"

Amy shook her head. "No, he travels around a lot and never stays in one place. He's a bit of a vagabond. Can't keep a job long enough to settle down. He sent me an email awhile back. I think he mentioned where he lived, but I'm sure I deleted it."

"One last question about James. Do you think he's capable of killing Liz?"

Amy looked at Nana, then back to Woodford. In unison they both said, "YES!"

"Amy, do you have any recent photographs of James or Ricky?"

"After kicking James out, I wanted nothing to do with him, so I either cut him out of every picture or threw them out. Ricky didn't like to have his picture taken. He always said he was ugly. He wasn't, but that's the excuse he gave."

"Could you give me a description of both men?"

Nana chuckled, "If you've seen one Porter, you've seen them all. There's probably eight-to-ten Porters in Scott County alone. Every one of them is big and dumb as they come, some more so than others. All are at least six-two and mean as snakes. They'd rather fight than shake a man's hand. But that's just my opinion."

"Did Ricky serve in the military?" asked Woodford.

"This may sound odd, but I'm not really sure. We never talked about it. I was just a dumb kid that got hitched right out of college. Ricky was two years my junior. Soon after that, he took a sales job that took him out of the country, or so he said. But he'd be gone for two or three months at a time, come home and he's tanned, or has a limp, and never talked about where he'd been or what he did. I'm not sure what he sold but there was always money, lots and lots of money. I finally got tired of the lies, and I guess he got tired of me asking. So, we divorced, and danged if he doesn't up and give me everything except the shirt off his back."

Woodford noted that Nana had been quietly wringing her handkerchief as if she was trying to squeeze the last drop of sudsy water out of a dishcloth. He kept waiting for it. Waiting...waiting...

Finally, she burst out, "Detective, there's something I have to tell you." She glanced at Amy, then back to Woodford.

"About three, maybe four weeks ago, I overheard Lizzie crying. At first she wouldn't say what was wrong, but finally, she broke down and the story poured out. A friend, she wouldn't say who, tried to force himself upon her. She swore there was no sex, just fondling. She begged me not to tell her mom. We argued, but in the end, I agreed." Nana's voice turned into a rattler hiss when she added, "If that 'friend' is the one who did this to her I'll...I'll never forgive myself." Nana's gaze met Amy's again. "Honey, I'm so sorry."

The kerchief she'd been holding was in knots and soaked with tears by the time she'd finished.

When it came to women, Woodford was not Sigmund Freud. But he knew now was not a good time to continue the interview. So, he bid his farewell.

He softly closed the door behind him and slowly walked to his car with a heavy heart.

As he sat behind the wheel, he debated as to which Porter might have killed Lizzie. James or Ricky? Or some other Porter? Or no Porter at all?

CHAPTER 15

Wednesday, July 7th

From the second-floor south window, Jane could see the Mississippi where a flotilla of sailboats jostled for position as they raced around the buoys. This momentary pause took her mind off the grislier business of checking the images of Lizzie's dead body. She and CSI Tom Perdan finished going over the stills and videos of the crime scene. She checked them again after he left.

A sign hung above her desk. "*Anything done once can be better served if thoroughly done right a second time.*" A motto she lived by.

Brian tapped on the metal doorframe with his Dr. Pepper can. "Finding anything new?" he mumbled through a mouth full of tuna sandwich.

She gave him a sideward glance and turned back towards the window. "Detective Woodford, would you mind telling me where you were the morning of the murder?"

"I worked out at Gold's Gym like I do every morning. Why?"

Jane paused for effect before continuing. "We found a thumb print in the blood next to Lizzie's body." She handed Woodford an 8x10 image. "Notice the scar on the inside of the thumb. Look familiar?"

Brian didn't even have to look. At age 13, he and a friend jumped a barbwire fence to get into the neighbor's yard. He sliced his thumb to the bone and it never healed properly, probably because he never told his parents. Old Smokey's yard was off limits and a good beating would be his if his Papa ever found out.

Of course, it was his thumb print. How careless.

"Cat got your tongue? Or are you waiting to lawyer up?"

"Call Gold's Gym...forget it. You're wasting our time. You know I didn't kill her. I must have forgotten to put on gloves before examining her body."

Jane couldn't hold in the belly laugh any longer and let out a hefty howl. "Ok, I believe you, but Perdan still thinks you're a viable suspect."

"Oh, he does, does he? You're a joke, Perdan," he yelled down the hall.

Brian wiped a spot of mayo off his tie and settled into his chair. "Did you get a chance to check on Tillie this morning?"

"I did, but she was pretty much out of it. How'd your interview with Mrs. Porter go?"

Woodford removed his notes and recorder from his pocket and set them on the desk. "I learned a lot and I gotta tell yah...well, just listen and let me know what you think."

Brian hit the play button and the tick tock of the grandfather's clock could be heard before Woodford began his interview.

***

Jane sat with her head in her hands, eyes closed, concentrating on every syllable of every word. When the tape finished, she replayed it, this time listening for deviations or tonal qualities that did not match the seriousness of Amy and Nana's stories. It became abundantly clear the two women were deeply in love with Lizzie. They were undeniably speaking the truth.

James Porter, she decided, was unquestionably a scumbag, but was he a murderer? No denying he held the skill set to pull off a murder of this nature. But his own daughter? Unless, of course, he found out the child belonged to his cousin Ricky. That would set off any sane man, and if the killer exhibited the same temper as James, no telling what that person was capable of doing.

Ricky Porter was a queer one. Who gives everything to the nagging wife unless he had something to hide? And where did he go for months at a time? And where did he get his money, and why wouldn't he talk about it? Ricky was a big question mark, with no answers.

Then there was the secret that someone molested Liz. That revelation most definitely needed to be considered. Did the pervert who molested Liz become paranoid and panic that Liz might tell all, setting him up for a lifetime in prison? Would that be enough to send a man over the edge to commit such horrendous acts of cruelty?

All three were viable suspects and Jane, who never jumped to conclusions without being 100% sure of her findings, wasn't about to fall into Brian's trap. Especially after the ribbing she'd just given him.

"Brian, I could make a strong case against all three men. But any good defense lawyer would chew me up and spit me out. Do I lean towards one...maybe, but not until I find out who this friend named Billy is. Right now, I feel he has the strongest motive to kill Liz. The Porters are...different, and I would never take them out of my sights. So, boss, I take it you have a favorite?"

Brian shrugged. "According to Amy, James Porter has a mean streak about him. He's a trained killer and has proven he will not hesitate to strike if he's provoked. So, yes. I'll take the obvious, and if I ever get my hands on James I won't hesitate to cuff him and bring him in for questioning. Jane, do what you so expertly do, and find this Billy. I'll do the same on the Porters. And tell

Perdan that if he thinks he's going to *pursue* me as a suspect, he might want to *pursue* another line of work."

Perdan, who'd been standing within earshot, made a mad dash to his cubical before he needed to come face to face with his boss.

CHAPTER 16

Wednesday, July 7th

Who was this Billy? Jane mused over this thought as she imagined a bullseye on Billy's back, and she in charge of target practice. She drummed her fingertips on her desk. Billy didn't know it yet but his life was about to become a living hell.

Becky Ahlstrom, Tillie's co-worker at Younkers, became rattled when Jane first interviewed her, and Sue Hatfield knew more than she let on. She and Tillie were best friends and cross country training partners. What did she know that would scare her so much that she wouldn't help out her best friend? Perhaps, she too, was molested by Billy?

All these thoughts and much more filled the white board in Jane's office: names, numbers, photos, and gut feels. The board reflected Jane's personality, thorough and uncluttered.

"Google...what is the phone number for Younkers in Davenport, Iowa?"

"The phone number for Younkers is...555-388-0000."

Jane jotted this on the board, then tapped the number on the phone screen. Two rings later an actual person answered. Jane was so shocked she almost forgot why she called.

Detective McCreary introduced herself and asked if she could

speak to a Becky. "I believe she works in Jewelry," Jane suggested.

Moments later, Becky came on the line.

"Hello?"

"Becky, it's Detective McCreary. We talked earlier. I really need your help."

Silence ensued.

"Detective...I'm scared. Please leave me alone." Becky hung up.

Jane sat there, the buzz of the dial tone ringing in her ear. She repeated the process for Sue Hatfield at Emeis golf course. Sue just finished work, and according to Ronnie, the club pro, decided to play a quick nine before heading home. Ronnie provided Jane with Sue's numbers, but even Jane, hack that she was, knew better than to call a player in the middle of a round. Instead she'd try and time it so she could meet Sue at the club house as she finished her round.

Jane's stomach grumbled like a mid-summer storm. She checked her watch and figured she'd have time for a sit-down lunch at the Rusty Nail and still make it to Younkers and have a heart-to-heart with Becky before Sue finished her nine. If the service was fast she might even have time to swing by and check in on Tillie.

Service was slow, very slow. But the Prime Rib sandwich she ordered was thick and juicy and the crinkle-cut fries were cooked to perfection. It was more than enough to stop the summer storm within.

She called for her check and paid in cash. Next stop, Younkers.

Jane watched Becky showing a sapphire necklace and earrings to an elderly gentleman who seemed to be in no hurry. Eventually, he did crack open his wallet and paid with cash. Jane wondered who the lucky lady was, until a platinum blond, half the man's age, shimmied up to her boyfriend.

McCreary waited off to the side by the perfume counter until Becky closed out the sale. As Jane approached, Ahlstrom recognized her from their earlier meeting and turned as red as the lipstick the blond left on the old man's forehead.

Jane tried gentle persuasion, to no avail. Threats of jail time, meaningless. No threats, prodding, or sweet-talking could make Becky give up something she didn't know. What little she knew, she shared and promised that if she remembered anything else she would give Jane a call.

As Jane started to leave, she noticed tears forming in Becky's eyes. She realized Becky wanted to help, but likely feared ending up like Liz. Next time she'd definitely need to formulate a new approach.

That is not how Jane pictured it would go. She checked her watch and realized she had about fifteen minutes to get over to Emeis and catch up with Sue Hatfield.

Sue completed her round of golf in less than an hour and was long gone by the time Jane arrived. Sue would be working the following morning and Jane planned on being there nice and early.

The bulls-eye on Billy's back was getting smaller and smaller, but still a target that Jane could not miss.

***

Ten minutes later Jane softly tapped on the door to Tillie's hospital room and gently pushed it open. Standing next to Tillie's bed was a slightly built, very attractive, forty-something blond and a Hulkish, six foot-four, behemoth of a man.

Jane introduced herself to Donna and David Silvermann. The ex-pro-linebacker crushed her hand like an empty beer can, but his sheepish smile belied the hate seething within.

As she flexed her fingers to get the blood flowing, Jane turned her attention to their daughter. The left side of Tillie's face displayed a palette of blues and deep purples. Her left eye was swollen shut and her lips, puffy as marshmallows, were trying to hold onto a red and white striped straw.

"Daanks," came a garbled thank you, as Tillie handed her mother the Styrofoam cup she'd been drinking from.

Dr. Oberhaus entered. "A good afternoon to you, Tillie, and how's my favorite patient on this beautiful day?" It was meant to be rhetorical, but Tillie managed to say, "Fine," which brought a broad smile to the doctor's face.

"Folks, could you give me a minute? I need to check her vitals, then you may step back in."

As the threesome exited to the waiting room, Jane was hit with an avalanche of questions. David needed answers and would not be denied. He wanted to kill the bastard that caused these injuries to his daughter.

David leaned against a wall. His fingers drummed an undistinguishable tune while his right foot tapped to the eerie beat. Anger seeped from his body like sweat on a hundred-degree day.

With time his breathing returned to normal and his attitude tempered as he listened to

Jane recount the story of how Tillie barely escaped death's deadly grip.

"David, your little girl was a hero. She fought off her attacker and stabbed him with a key." Upon hearing this, he smiled, a deep smile that stretched across his broad face. "That's my girl."

Jane saw tears of pride well up in his eyes. She paused to allow the magnitude of what they'd heard to settle in before resuming.

Jane skipped over Tillie's time in the water. Mostly because no one knew what happened during her time in Duck Creek. She resumed her telling of the ordeal with Dusty Andrews finding Tillie clinging to a fallen tree:

"Folks, what I'm going to tell you next is what movies are made of. We know for a fact that Tillie lay in Duck Creek for several hours. By some fortuitous stroke of luck or God extending his hand, a young man, Dusty Andrews, came upon a blond mannequin entangled in a fallen tree. In his exact words he said, '*It would look cool in my dorm room.*' He proceeded to lie on the ground, stretching to grab the blond hair."

"A mannequin! Where was Tillie?" exclaimed Donna.

"Well, imagine Dusty's shock as he grabbed a handful of hair and Tillie let out a terrifying scream. In his panic, he lost his grip on the tree root and tumbled into the water, losing his camera and phone in his urgency to rescue your screaming daughter.

"Somehow, he managed to untangle Tillie's water logged body from the tree branches and together they floated downstream before finding a place to exit. He carried her two blocks back to his truck and delivered her to the emergency entrance here at Genesis. A true, bonafide hero."

Through sobs of joy, Donna asked, "Will we ever get to meet Tillie's savior?"

"I'm sure you will."

As their conversation was coming to an end, Tillie's door edged open and Dr. Oberhaus paused to speak with them.

"Folks, Tillie's very weak. So, Jane, you've got five minutes, no more. Understand?"

Jane nodded her acceptance and entered to find Tillie's fingers prodding her battered face. A muted "Why?" was all that she uttered. No training at the academy prepared Jane for that simple three-letter question. How could they?

"Tillie, do you remember much about what happened? Or what your attacker looked like?"

Silence, then a flash of an idea.

"I vaguely remember stabbing my attacker, I think?" Tillie paused, as another thought crossed her mind. "In my dreams, images of the man's face burst like fireworks before vanishing into a smoky haze." The last few words were barely audible.

Tillie took a deep breath, her eyes rolled back into her head and her body slid down between the covers. A soft rumbling came from deep inside her. Her eyes popped open, and darted around the room. "Don't let him hurt me, Mommy! Don't let him hurt me."

Just as quickly, she was gone again. Perhaps deep, deep into her memory where her assailant dwells.

Realizing little else would be forthcoming, Jane ended the interview with a kiss to Tillie’s forehead and a promise of justice.

CHAPTER 17

Wednesday, July 7th

The one-story ranch looked nothing like Amy Porter's immaculate, well-maintained home. It needed a coat of paint and new shingles. The gutters dangled freely and were in peril of falling. Due to the lack or unwillingness to maintain the grounds, a wooded park that abutted the backyard was taking over ownership. For all intents and purposes the house appeared abandoned, much like the rest of the block.

Detectives Charlie Owens and Harold Steinman held out little hope of finding Patty Sue Porter home. If it wasn't for the ninety-something Crown Vic in the drive, they wouldn't have bothered to knock.

"This is a waste of our time," said Owens and the two detectives turned to leave.

Footsteps and the creak of the front door opening stopped them in their tracks.

Patty Sue Porter, Ricky's second wife, opened the door and stepped out on the landing. She wore a flimsy pink robe open from her shoulders to her knees, exposing her ample breasts and much, much more. A cigarette dangled from her nicotine-stained left hand. A can of Bud occupied her right. She perked up when she saw the two handsome men standing before her.

"What can I do for you gentlemen? You here for business or pleasure?"

"Excuse me, ma'am, would you mind closing your robe?" asked Owens.

Patty Sue smiled a shit eating grin. "Would you mind holding these?"

Neither could keep their eyes from drifting to the brunette's cleavage.

"I'm referring to my cigarette and beer, you silly boys." With her hands now free, she gently caressed both breasts. "I don't charge for looking." None-the-less, she pulled the top of her robe closed.

The two detectives finally introduced themselves. Steinman, being the senior of the two, took charge.

"Could we have a couple minutes of your time? Is Ricky Porter home?"

"Ricky's off fishing with his buddies. Or so he says."

Peggy Sue abruptly turned and reentered the house, her robe flapping in the breeze. "Are you boys going to just stand there or are you coming in?"

The two detectives glanced at one another, shrugged and followed. They were somewhat surprised. The interior looked relatively neat and tidy, nothing like the exterior.

Patty Sue excused herself and came back dressed in a Van Halen t-shirt and cut-offs. She must have run a brush through her hair because she transformed from a tramp into a soccer mom. That was until she opened the fridge, pulled out a beer and tapped a Camel from a half-empty pack. After accepting a light from Owens, she took a deep drag and blew smoke rings across the room. "So how can I help you boys?"

Ten minutes later, Steinman and Owens thanked Patty Sue and headed for their car, none the wiser.

"You all come back if you want a good time!" she called out after them. A puff of smoke was all that remained as the door closed behind them.

"So, Charlie. What do you think?"

"I think...I won't come back alone. That's what I think. What about you, Steinman? You coming back?"

Steinman looked back at the house and saw Peggy Sue staring through the parted curtains. "No, I think I like my job too much."

As they pulled out of the drive, Ricky Porter appeared from the back bedroom. He approached his wife and grabbed her ass.

"Do you think they believed me?" she said.

"Sweet Cheeks, they were so mesmerized by your boobs, you could have told them the world was flat and cows don't fart. They swallowed it hook line and sinker. It's time to pack."

***

Back at the office, Woodford was also looking into Ricky Porter. Follow the money. That mantra always served him well. But, before he could dig into Ricky's financials, the muffled ring tone of his cell went off deep in his pants pocket. After fumbling through four rings, he finally extracted the phone. It was Amy Porter.

He found a quiet space just around the corner from his office and leaned up against the wall. Amy called to confirm she'd indeed deleted the email James sent. However, she did discover two faded pictures of Ricky with his fishing buddies, but none of James. This seemed to brighten her mood.

Woodford thanked her for the update and then asked how she was holding up.

"Oh, I guess as well as can be expected. Nana made me a tuna salad sandwich for lunch. I ate most of it, but I didn't really feel hungry."

"A tuna sandwich is what I ate. Tuna has always been a favorite ever since I was...well, knee high to a grasshopper."

That brought a chuckle as Amy whimsically answered, "Mine too."

Woodford knew how to be a good listener. It was part of his job description. He slid down the wall and sat cross-legged as Amy regaled in whimsical tales of Lizzie's childhood. With each remembrance, her mood changed. There were signs of a lilt in her voice and she even giggled as she reminisced about the time she and Lizzie caught Santa stuffing a pillow under his suit. Lizzie cried for days because she thought she'd only get coal for being such a bad girl.

The longer Brian listened, the more he realized how attached he was to Amy Porter. The fires from long ago were beginning to flare-up. It was a good feeling, one he hadn't felt since his high school days. A feeling he needed to squash, until they at least put the killer behind bars.

His phone chirped, a reminder he was running low on power. So, he bid Amy farewell and promised he'd be in contact soon. A smile crept across his face as he closed his phone and slid it back into his pocket.

CHAPTER 18

Wednesday, July 7th

Rick Gonzales, manager of Midwest Wheel and Rim, was beginning to worry about his number one driver, Raymond Hund. Until now Hund never missed a day's work without calling in. He tried Hund's cell but no answer. So, he took the short drive to Hund's place but found no one home. A huge shipment was scheduled to go out in two days and Ray was the only one licensed to drive an 18-wheeler. He'd give him one more day and then he'd call the police.

CHAPTER 19

Several months earlier

Planning for East's 20th high school reunion fell on the shoulders of Tim Cain, Roger Timberline, Mary Lou Townsman, and Jackie Petersen. They were able to contact all but 24 of their former classmates and 182 of the Bull's faithful agreed to come to some or all of the three planned events.

Thursday evening, July 8th, would be a casual gathering at the Circle Tap. Most of the locals and even some of the out-of-towners agreed they'd make this event. There was going to be plenty of cold beer, great ribs, and a lot of camaraderie. All were encouraged to bring their yearbooks and memories.

On Friday, a much-anticipated golf outing at the Davenport Country Club was planned, with prizes galore. Afterwards, they would meet at the Rhythm City Casino for a chance to try out Lady Luck.

On Saturday, a flotilla would form at Credit Island and float down the Mississippi, ending with a cookout at Buffalo Shore Park. Later that evening everyone would meet at the Fair Grounds for karaoke, dancing and a lot of partying. Hopefully the weather would be sunny and the rain would stay away.

CHAPTER 20

Thursday, July 8th

McCreary arrived at her desk around 7:15, a little early even for her. To call Jane an over-achiever would be an understatement. She was relentless in her pursuit of perfection.

As Jane thought about the events of the past two days, she recalled an incident that occurred near the end of her third year on the force. A nasty murder of a family had happened in the Gold Coast area of Davenport.

The Booker clan had gone to bed early to get a good night's sleep before they left the next morning on a long-awaited vacation to Disney Land. Days later, parents, Fran and Darrin, were found nude and taped to kitchen chairs. Both were tortured repeatedly over a three-day period. Fran had been brutally raped, as was her 14-year-old daughter, Brandy, who lay spread eagled and naked in front of her parents. Eight-year-old BJ heard his family screaming and managed to sneak into his closet and hide in a basket of dirty laundry undetected. Several times he'd heard the men calling his name and taunting him, but he stayed hidden in his cramped quarters. Late at night he'd sneak out, stretch, and nibble on left over Halloween candy, but never left the closet for fear of being caught. Late on the third day BJ heard the pop, pop, pop of a revolver, then the slamming of a door. He stayed put for another hour and then snuck out of his hiding place, only to find his entire family murdered.

Two months passed with nary a clue. Jane was relentless. She spent many untold hours poring over what little intel they'd collected. One evening, late in the second month of the investigation, Jane found herself scouring through the family garbage for easily the third time. Once again, she took out the usual collection of fast-food containers, dirty paper plates covered with mold, and several Pepsi cans. She took each can and vigorously shook it while listening for a telltale sign of a hidden clue. During the shaking of a third can Jane detected something bouncing around inside. Whatever was hiding within the aluminum walls would not shake free. She retrieved an electric opener from the break room, and was beyond excited as the opener slowly inched its way around to its starting point. A dried-up cigarette butt fell to the counter. None of the Booker family smoked, so she immediately contacted her superior, Detective Woodford, and informed him of her discovery. It took another two weeks for the DNA found on the butt to be identified.

Three months to the day of the murders, the SWAT team swarmed the dwelling of Brad Kopatch, a disgruntled ex-employee of Darrin's. Eventually, Brad gave up the names of his accomplices and they were able to close the case.

Due to her diligence and dedication, not only to this case but to every case she'd ever worked, Jane received her detective's badge. This came one month shy of her 30th birthday, making her the youngest and only female homicide detective on the Davenport Police force.

A large red exercise ball that Jane used for a chair sat next to the filing cabinet. She rolled it in front of her desk, sat down, bounced a couple of times, and began her daily routine by checking her inbox for the morning's hot sheet. Thankfully it was clear of murders, but once again a Kwik Shop had been burglarized just north of interstate 280 on the outskirts of Davenport. Like the previous burglaries, the description of the thief was similar, right down to the Yankee's ball cap.

Even though a homicide didn't happen, Jane felt it could turn into one. After this last robbery, she decided to talk to Woodford, and if he'd agree, she'd take the lead on this case, even if it meant stepping on Sergeant Hawthorne's toes. Hopefully he'd understand.

But first, she wanted to make contact with Tillie.

Jane punched in the number for Tillie's room and was greeted by Donna Silvermann.

"Good morning, Donna, it's Jane McCreary. How's Tillie?"

After a moment's hesitation she answered, "Tillie's better physically, I suppose. The swelling is going down and the pain is diminishing. But, mentally...she's extremely depressed."

There was a lull, as if neither knew quite what to say.

As if ordained, Dr. Oberhaus entered the room.

"Jane, Dr. Oberhaus just arrived. Would you like to speak to him?

***

"Jane, you there?"

"I'm here. How's our girl doing, doctor?"

"Tillie is healing nicely. She has passed all the concussion protocols, and I'm predicting that within the week she'll be back to her vibrant self. As for the amnesia, I compare her mind to a blank canvas waiting for an image to appear, one stroke at a time. Only the artist knows when he's ready."

McCreary thanked him for the update, said goodbye, and hung up.

Next on her to-do list was a visit to Emeis Golf Course to talk with Sue Hatfield. She hoped that a little face-to-face time would encourage Sue to be forthcoming. Otherwise, their battle would make the Hatfield and McCoy's odyssey look like a cake walk.

CHAPTER 21

Thursday, July 8th

Woodford made his appearance at 8:00 A.M. and went straight to the lounge for coffee and a glazed doughnut.

Before he could even sip his coffee and take a bite of his favorite breakfast, Jane cornered him.

"Brian, you got a minute?"

"Make it quick. My coffee's getting cold. Want one?"

"No thanks. Listen, yesterday there was another Kwik Shop robbery. This time our perp displayed a knife. I firmly believe that our murder case and these robberies are the work of the same man. Any chance you'd change your mind and let me take a stab at the robberies? Pun intended."

Woodford spun around a couple of times in his chair before replying. "Jane, the man displayed a knife. I get it. He has the same physical attributes as our killer. And these crimes took place basically during the same time frame. However, I just don't see how these crimes tie together. Is there something I'm missing?"

"No, that's pretty much it. I could play devil's advocate, however, and suggest that our Kwik Shop robber would be a complete fool for killing Lizzie and then stick around and rob multiple stores. But let's look at it from another angle. Maybe, just maybe, someone hires an assassin to knock off Liz but lacked the funds to seal the contract. I know it's a scenario that sounds farfetched, but it's something that needs to be looked into, and I'm the gal to get it done."

Woodford took a couple more spins in his chair and finally agreed. He always found it hard to argue with Jane. She was his favorite and a damn fine detective to boot. Besides, he owed her multiple favors.

Woodford spotted Squid standing in the doorway but chose not to explain why he had a change of heart. His decision would stand.

As Woodford stood and began inspecting the sticky notes stuck to his computer screen, white slivers of frosting on his shirt fell into the controls. He flipped the keyboard and gave it a hearty shake. Multi-colored crumbs from past dietary delights littered his desk. He gathered them together like lost sheep, licked his pointer finger and dabbed at the mystery concoctions.

"Disgusting!" Jane nearly gagged.

A lavender note attached to his computer screen advised him to call Midwest Wheel and Rim and ask for Rick Gonzales. An employee was missing for the past two days and Gonzales worried there might be foul play involved.

Squid sucked up his courage and walked into the office.

Woodford handed him the note. "Give Gonzales a call and see what's going on. Thanks." Brian licked his finger once again and dabbed at the remaining multi-colored flakes.

***

Squid, in a fit of anger, intentionally bumped into McCreary. "Here," and handed her a quarter inch-thick manila folder containing three days of painstaking meticulous work he'd put in on the Kwik shop robberies. "I hope you choke on it."

"Ouch." It wasn't the bump. That she could take in spades and give back double. No, it was the rejection. She liked Squid, perhaps more than anyone else in the office. She'd have to find a way to repay him.

"You wanted the case. Now you got it," said Woodford. He knew Squid's anger was a double-edged sword. One side was meant for him, the other reserved for Jane.

Woodford turned and gave Jane the cold shoulder.

Double ouch.

CHAPTER 22

Thursday, July 8th

Brian punched in "9" for Amy Porter.

On the fifth ring Amy answered. Brian took this as a good sign. After the usual banter, Woodford got to the point of the call.

"Amy, we've been unable to make contact with James. Is there anything - anything at all - you can remember that might help us locate him?"

"Detective, after we talked last night, I seemed to remember James saying something in his email about being in town this weekend for his high school reunion. Do you think I should be worried?"

Woodford promised he'd put extra patrols in her neighborhood. "I'm also sending an officer over to pick up Lizzie's computer and cell phone." As an after-thought he added, "If you'd like, I'm free tonight and can stop by.

I have a few more questions about Ricky and James."

"What a lovely offer. I'd love to have you come by this evening, and I'd feel so much safer. Would 7:00 be okay?"

This brought a smile to his face, and he thought, *Now this is a woman I would change my life for.* What the heck was he thinking, change his life? *Well, yes…definitely, yes.*

He wanted to get this new information out right away. So, he apologized to Amy for not being able to chat longer. He said his goodbye, and without putting down the phone, placed a call to Trent Buckley, who was pulling desk duty for the month of July.

"Buckley, I need you to place extra patrols in the Porter's neighborhood starting immediately! It's possible James Porter could be in town for his high school reunion. Remind the boys our suspect was Special Forces. Need I say more?"

After hanging up Woodford walked into the lounge and found Zoe Wilson, Hawthorne's partner. "I need you to go over to Porter's and pick up their computers, laptops, and phones. Have the lab sweep them for anything dealing with either of the Porter cousins or a Billy. I think we're on to something here, so tell them to put a rush on it."

Returning to his office, he placed a call to Clint Ashford, East High's track coach. On the third ring a sexy voice identified herself as Ashford's wife. She explained that Clint was out of town for several track seminars at Iowa State, in Ames, Iowa, but promised to return home early once he'd heard of Lizzie's death.

Woodford gave her his number and requested that Clint call him upon his return. After hanging up he thought, *I have got to see the woman behind that voice.*

He gave his head a mighty shake. *Brian, Brian, Brian. One minute you're thinking of spending the rest of your life with Amy, the next you're lusting after a voice on the phone.* "Rat...a fully pedigreed rat," he turned and checked out the room. Thankfully no one heard his little outburst.

CHAPTER 23

Thursday, July 8th

Detective Woodford stood in the far south corner of the main office staring out the window at nothing. He was exhausted. He took the penny he found earlier out of his pocket. *Come on little penny, bring me some luck.*

As Woodford turned back to his desk, his secretary raised two fingers. "Line two."

"Woodford, it's Hawthorne. You and McCreary need to get over to Raymond Hund's place. I think I found our murder suspect!"

"WHAT?"

"Just get over here! It doesn't get any better than this!"

Woodford placed the call to McCreary, and after disconnecting, grabbed his GLOCK and badge and bolted for the door.

***

Jane was on her way to the scene of the third Kwik shop robbery when she received the call, but after hearing the news she hit the brakes and made a screeching U-turn in the middle of Highway 6, leaving S-shaped strips of black rubber behind her. By the time she reached Wisconsin Avenue, the needle read ninety. She jerked the wheel hard right and fishtailed onto Wisconsin, just missing an oncoming semi.

***

The gravel road leading to the white clapboard house was a good quarter mile long. Sergeant Hawthorne dodged multiple potholes before reaching the home of Raymond Hund.

The exterior hadn't seen a brush of paint in decades. The house was in such disarray that the front porch looked to be listing by twenty degrees and ready to drown in a patch of thistles the size of a Sherman tank.

The six windows fronting the two-story house were either covered with discolored rotting plywood or contained broken panes of glass shot out by vandals. The yard was littered with rusted out shells of abandoned vehicles, ancient farm equipment, and under an old lean-to, a neglected lawn mower that hadn't seen the light of day in twenty years. The unattached garage was in even worse disrepair. Holes the size of basketballs dotted the moss-covered roof. The door, however, looked to be recently replaced.

Sergeant Hawthorne worked his way up the weed-strewn footpath and through toys of Christmas past. Avoiding all the landmines, he finally reached and climbed onto the rickety old porch, each step a new adventure.

He rapped on the only pane of glass that was not cracked or broken and each time came a hollow empty reply. He tried the doorknob and found it locked. *Why would anyone bother to lock up this piece of junk?* He could only imagine.

The adventure of retracing his steps was fraught with rusted beer cans, broken bottles and the occasional snake. One, a colorful species, hissed as it crawled across his boot. Damn, he hated snakes and this was a big one. Upon reaching the surprisingly clutterless driveway, he worked his way to the back of the house.

The rear door displayed a recent paint job and all the glass panes were shiny and new. He took a moment to survey his surroundings before rapping on one of the panes. The hollow sounds reverberated throughout the house. He pressed his cupped hands against one of the windows. His nose touched the cold pane of glass. It was not what he saw, but what he smelled that made him take a hasty step backwards. A smell he knew all too well as rotting flesh.

He tried turning the brass knob, but like the front door, it too was locked.

Using the butt of his baton, Hawthorne smashed one of the small panes and reached through to unlock the door. He un-holstered his sidearm and slowly inched the door open.

Staring back at him were two pairs of un-blinking, un-wavering dark eyes. The two rodents, rats by the look of their size, double dared Hawthorne to enter their abode.

Reaching to his right, he found a switch. The bright light caused the two rats to blink, and then scurry to the back of the refrigerator.

He placed the crook of his left arm over his nose and mouth and took one step into the kitchen and stopped.

The kitchen looked fairly modern considering the exterior of the place. All the appliances were relatively new and the room was obviously just wallpapered. What a shame the owner would not be able to enjoy the labors of his work, assuming the decomposing body was Raymond Hund.

The eyes of the dead man were eaten away, likely by the two rats whose pointy little noses were now sticking out from behind the stove. A gaping wound, just below the man's shirt collar, exhibited a feeding ground for flies and larvae.

His stomach could take no more.

As he stepped backwards out the door, the two rats made a beeline for their early morning meal. Hawthorne wanted to put a bullet between their beady little eyes. Instead, he removed his cell phone and called headquarters.

***

Moments later, the first car, with sirens blaring, came crashing over the potted driveway with little or no care for its under-carriage.

With evidence bag in tow, Detective McCreary climbed out of the car and hoofed it towards the back yard where Squid stood waving.

From twenty feet, Jane caught the telltale odor of rotting flesh. Stopping, she unzipped her bag and pulled out a jar of Vaseline. She placed a healthy gob of the yellow cream under her nose and offered the jar to Hawthorne.

"I suppose you want to take charge of this crime?" asked Squid.

"No, Woodford will take charge when he gets here and you know that. You'll get the credit where credit is due. Look, I'm sorry if I stepped on your toes, but my gut feeling told me all along that whoever keeps robbing the Kwik Shops is Lizzie's killer. Perhaps I was wrong. My apologies."

"Let's get to work," said Squid, and the two officers took a step into the kitchen. The rats once again found their favorite hiding place behind the stove and were daring each other to race back out and snatch another bite. Instead, they skittered across the floor, and were heading out the door when Jane's right heel stomped down on the skull of one of the rodents. Crunch, crunch, crackle.

"You're lucky, Squid, I just saved your life." The critter, dangling by its tail, was carried to a rusted-out garbage bin. Jane brushed her hands against her pants before heading back to the house and the dead body. "Done."

After a snicker or two their attention returned to the dead victim and the demanding task of securing the crime scene.

At the top of her pad Jane placed the date, Thursday, July 8th, the time, 10:38 A.M and in large block letters wrote RAYMOND HUND???

Just then they heard a light tap on the door.

"Okay to come in?" asked CSI agents Perdan and Tandy. With nary a nod, Jane returned to her sketch of the kitchen and the juxtaposition of the dead body and furnishings.

Perdan entered, removed his Nikon from its case, and began circling the kitchen capturing every nuance of their crime scene. Jane preferred the tried and true pencil and sketchpad. Tom preferred digital imagery. Together they missed nothing.

***

Woodford arrived moments later, quickly processed the room with his photographic mind, and shook his head.

He was a patient man if nothing else. But today his inner-self screamed at him. *Nothing about this crime scene holds true.* It reeked of falsehoods and not just the pungent smell of their dead victim.

"Be patient grasshopper," he said to no one in particular. So, he sat back and waited, flipping a shiny penny until his crew finished. Then and only then would he listen to what they'd found.

Tick...Tock...Tick...Tock

Jane detected the anxiety emanating from her boss, but before she could ask what troubled him, coroner Dr. Ball stuck his head through the door.

"You guys talking about me? My nose is itching."

Stopping dead in his tracks, Ball gave a soft whistle. "Now that's something you don't see every day."

Not one to waste time, Ball closed in and began examining the body.

Patrick, his assistant, began gathering the maggots and larvae.

"These little critters are as good at conveying the time of death as any modern technology," stated Ball.

Dr. Ball motioned for Jane to come over. "Jane, do you see the trails left by the maggots in the blood? We call these trails Maggot Monet's."

"Doc, they're kind of cool, in an artistic abstract kind of way," said Jane, as she wrinkled her nose in disgust.

Ball paced around the corpse, tilting his head to and fro for a good look, before moving to another angle for a different perspective.

He took a tongue depressor out of his bag and began examining the eyes.

"Rats! Big as squirrels," chipped in Hawthorne.

"Thought as much. With this heat, it made for a tasty meal they couldn't resist," said Ball.

Next, he gently pressed the tongue depressor in and around the shoulder wound. "It's not a through and through, so no bullet caused this wound. A key. Don't know, maybe?" He was having a dialogue with himself at this point. "I'll have to get him under a microscope to be sure."

He picked up the right hand. "Definitely blood under the nails. Don't know whose." He was talking to himself again.

"Brian, you and your team done with the victim? Not much more I can do here."

"Well, Doc, it depends. Can you give me an estimate on height and weight and time of death? I've got some thoughts rattling around in this old brain that could use some input."

"You're not asking for much."

Doc pinched his lips together and made a smacking noise. "Height, I'd guess 5'11, tops. Weight, no idea at all. He's too bloated to even hazard a guess. The maggots tell me he's been dead about two days. As always, let's put him on the table and I'll know more for sure."

There was a moment of silence just before CSI Tandy walked into the room. "Boss, found a wallet in the bedroom with a driver's license belonging to our missing Raymond Hund."

After checking the ID for height and weight, Woodford handed the wallet back to Tandy. "Bag and tag, Sergeant."

Dr. Ball and his assistant secured the body and proceeded back to the lab, a trail of questions forming as unique as the Maggot Monet's.

While Detectives McCreary, Owens, Steinman and CSI agents Tandy and Perdan were sweeping the house for clues, Woodford exited the residence. His inquisitive mind wanted to see what details the garage might hold.

Inside, Woodford found what he was looking for: a dark blue Chevy van. His mind wasn't ready to accept that Raymond Hund was their killer. He had his reasons, but he wouldn't share those yet.

He didn't want prints of his thumb left at the crime scene again, so he put on latex gloves and opened the driver's side door. There were a few small smears of blood on the door handle and console but not nearly enough to cause the stench that enveloped the van.

He climbed in and was surprised to find he needed to stretch to reach the pedals. Whoever drove the van last had to be a good two to three inches taller than he.

One thing was for certain. If the man on the kitchen floor turned out to be Hund, he sure as hell didn't drive the van last.

Woodford twisted in the seat and looked into the rear compartment. It looked like a scene from the TV show "Hoarders." A seasonal collection of clothing was scattered all over the floor. Work boots, jogging shoes, slippers, basically someone's whole wardrobe. Tying it all together was a coating of blood.

Reaching back, he pulled out a red, XXX flannel shirt, and a pair of wrangler jeans, size 38 waist with an in-seam of 36. He'd seen enough. Time to lock it up and let the experts disseminate the evidence. His last thought: *The killer definitely drove this van.*

Before heading back to the house, he checked the glove box and found registration and insurance papers for a Holly Jorgensen of Chicago, not Raymond Hund of Davenport. "Hmmm."

As he exited the garage, Woodford placed a call to the DMV. He got Holly's phone information and tried calling. It went straight to voice mail. *They always go straight to voice mail.* He cursed.

Re-entering the house, he cornered Hawthorne and told him about the van. "I want you to get that van down to the station and have them go over it with a fine-toothed comb. Our killer drove that vehicle and I want to know who it is. Capiche?"

"Woodford! Got a minute?" It was McCreary.

"Boss, we just finished dusting for prints. This place is spotless. No prints on anything, none, zip, zero. Look at this room and tell me if that's not the strangest thing you've ever seen."

"Yeah, a real Ripley's Believe It or Not," said Woodford. "Jane, I'm going to run something past you, and if you think I'm full of it just kick me in the ass and send me on my way. Tuesday, Liz Porter is murdered and Tillie stabs said killer. She's thrown into the creek to die but survives. The killer takes off in a blue van, which I just found parked in Hund's garage. We find a dead body with a neck wound, but he hardly fits the profile of our killer. We can assume the dead man is Hund but not the bike-path butcher. So, who's the killer?"

Jane shakes her head. "Please continue, oh wise one."

"I'll tell you who he is. He's a psychopathic killer. Now here's what I think. Our killer comes here for help and Hund stiches or patches him up and he survives. And for a job well done, our perp stabs Hund, probably with a key to try and throw us off. To make things worse the van belongs to a Holly Jorgensen of Chicago, who's also probably dead. You know what I need? A drink. Care to join me?"

Jane checked her watch. "Hardly time for a scotch on the rocks. Besides, I still need to catch up with Sue Hatfield and look in on Tillie."

"Sounds good. Great job, team. We're getting closer."

Brian went directly to his favorite watering hole.

***

Happy hour had just begun when he bellied-up to the bar. "A Dr. Pepper and some of those salted peanuts if you would, please."

Unconsciously, he wrinkled his nose and did a double sniff of the most powerful body odor he'd ever smelled. He coyly looked to his left and then right before realizing he was the culprit that was fowling the air. He tossed a crumpled up five-dollar bill on the old oak bar and fled for the nearest exit, his drink untouched.

As Brian showered, the stench of the morning rolled off him one droplet of death at a time.

The heat and steam of the pounding water against his face slowly began to relax his aching muscles, but not his mind. No, his mind kept returning to Liz Porter, with her emerald green eyes, and Raymond Hund, with no eyes at all.

CHAPTER 24

Thursday, July 8th

How long had his phone been ringing, five, six times? The turquoise towel dropped to the floor as he picked his phone off the dresser.

It was Clint Ashford, teacher and coach of the East High track team. The two agreed to meet at the station in an hour. It might be something or maybe nothing at all.

Brian was hopping around on one leg trying to pull on a pair of slacks when his phone rang a second time.

"Detective Woodford here. How can I help?"

"Brian, it's Amy Porter. I hate to bother you but I just heard on the radio that you caught Lizzie's killer. Is that true?"

"Amy..."

Hop, hop, hop...

"It's true, we do have..."

Hop, hop, hop...

"Hang on a sec, I need to put my pants on."

"Oh, Brian, you don't need to put pants on just to talk to me."

"Very funny. Hold on." *He knew there was a reason why he fell for this woman,* and chuckled as he continued to dress.

"Amy, it's true we did apprehend a suspect. Not that we needed cuffs. The man has been dead for at least a couple of days. We're fifty percent sure he's not Lizzie's killer, and one-hundred percent sure he knew our suspect in some kind of capacity. I can't tell you a whole lot more until we know for sure who our corpse is and how he ties in with this whole mess. I can tell you with great certainty that our dead man is not James or Ricky Porter."

"Oh, dear. That means James is still out there. Brian, should I worry?"

"Stay indoors, keep your shades pulled and doors locked. I've ordered extra security to patrol your block. But I really don't think you have to worry about James or Ricky. They may not be the nicest gentlemen in the world, but I don't think they're stupid enough to kill you or Nana. They have to know they're on our radar. So, relax and I'll be over in a couple of hours."

"If you say so. But I've known James and Ricky for a long time and if they want me dead, I'll be dead, locked doors or not. I'm sorry, detective, perhaps I'm just overly paranoid."

"Amy, you're not paranoid. Okay, a little paranoid maybe. And you have a right to be. Look, I have an interview with Coach Ashford and I still need to check in with our coroner to see what he's learned about our latest victim. So, if all goes well, I should still make it around seven-ish if that's ok?"

It was, and he bid farewell.

Instead of his power tie, he grabbed his Glock and badge off the counter, a much stronger statement than any neckwear.

Woodford checked his watch. Thirty-five minutes until his meeting with Coach Ashford. Time enough to check in with Dr. Ball.

CHAPTER 25

Thursday, July 8th

"Well, well, if it isn't the great Detective Brian Woodford. Impeccable timing, my friend. Have you come here to wow me with your supernatural detective skills, or do you need your lowly assistant to fill in some gaps for you?"

"Oh, wise and mighty coroner, I seek knowledge only you can provide. Tell me your findings and let me be on my way."

Both folded their hands and bowed at the waist.

"As you wish," said Ball.

Dan started ticking off his preliminary findings as Woodford retrieved two Pepsis from the fridge.

"The autopsy reveals several interesting facts," said Ball. "Prints confirmed my cadaver on the table is Hund. However, I wanted a positive ID so I called Rick Gonzales at Mid-West Wheel and Rim for facial recognition. He took one look at our deceased, turned green, and bolted for the door. We'll have to go with prints.

"Test results and our maggots put the time of death at approximately 5:00 P.M. last Tuesday evening. He died of a stab wound to the pectoral artery. But, thanks to our rat's eating habits, I'm afraid I'd lose the game of Clue if I declared that a key, in the kitchen, by Professor Plum was my who, what, and where of this murder." His attempt at humor didn't even crack a smile so he continued.

"Hund was five-eleven, hardly tall enough to make the cut that killed Liz Porter. Second, he was over-weight. He tipped the scales at 250, so chasing down Liz would have been virtually impossible. Third, the blood type found in the house did not match that at Tillie's crime scene. And fourth, I checked his fist for abrasions, and they're as soft and scar free as a baby's bottom. There's no way he hit Tillie hard enough to crack her cheek and jawbone without doing some kind of damage to his hand. Also, during his autopsy I found two newly broken ribs with very little bruising in and around the adjoining tissue. The indentations on the ribs and crescent shaped laceration to the skin indicate our victim was savagely kicked post-mortem.

"Brian, as much as I want it to be, Hund could not have committed that murder. But somebody sure has gone to a lot of trouble to make us think so. Hund was nothing more than a pawn in a deadly chess match.

"However, my friend, I am on to something that may pay dividends. I've been doing background checks on Hund and found out he was in the service. I checked his military records and he served as a medic in Afghanistan. Woodford, I'll bet the price of that Pepsi you're drinking that our killer came to Hund for help. Hund successfully closed the man's wound and died for his efforts. One hell of a friend, agreed?"

"Agreed, mi amigo."

Brian was proud of the work his buddy completed and didn't want to squash his enthusiasm by mentioning he'd come to the same conclusion.

Brian checked the clock on the wall and realized he was running late for his appointment with Coach Ashford. So, he guzzled the last of his Pepsi and threw a perfect spiral into the hands of Ball, just like their high school days.

CHAPTER 26

Thursday, July 8th

Back at the station, Brian poked his head into McCreary's office. "Jane, has Coach Ashford arrived?"

She pointed to the drinking fountain and indicated the ruggedly handsome man standing next to a much younger, equally attractive female.

"Mr. Ashford, I'm Detective Woodford. Would you please step into my office?"

"Should my wife join us?"

"Perhaps later, but for now you're the one I need to talk to."

Woodford closed the door behind him and offered Ashford a seat. "Can I get you something cold?"

"No, thanks."

"Mr. Ashford..."

"Please, call me Coach."

"Okay. Coach, do you teach at East High school?"

"Yes, PE and I coach cross-country as well as indoor and outdoor track."

"Coach, how many years have you worked at East High?"

"Let's see...this will be my ninth year."

"Did you teach anywhere else before being hired at East?"

"I've been in the Davenport School system going on 14 years now. The first five were at Wallace Intermediate School. When the East job opened, I jumped at the chance and never looked back."

"Coach, as you know, we are investigating the murder of Liz Porter. There are some questions that need to be asked so I can cross you off our suspect list. Do you understand?"

"Do I need a lawyer?"

"Not at this time. Do you think you need one?"

"Absolutely not! Liz ran track and cross-country at East High for the past three years. When you're around these kids for that long they become family. So please ask me anything.

Believe me, I want to catch this bastard far more than you ever will."

Ashford had been a guest speaker at the Ames Sports Clinic at the time of the murder, which was a rock-solid alibi. Still, Woodford collected names and numbers and would check to see if his alibi held true.

Basically, the interview was a bust and coach was clean as the whistle around his neck. Woodford was ready to call it a night, until he asked about any assistants that worked with Coach Ashford.

"Coach, Amy Porter says you have an assistant. What's his name?"

"Billy Perkins is my lead assistant for both track and cross-country." The names of the other coaches didn't even register a blip on Brian's radar screen once Billy's name was mentioned.

"Billy Perkins? How well do you know him, coach?"

"He's been my assistant for two years. He's a student at

St. Ambrose and, if I'm not mistaken, all he has left is his student teaching. I can't speak highly enough concerning his work and dedication to our program. He's never missed a single practice and works tirelessly to help the team succeed."

"Coach, how old would you guess Billy to be?"

"Let's see, he did two tours in the Marines right out of high school. Took one in the shoulder or probably would still be a jar head. HooRah. So, my guess would be late twenties, early thirties."

"Does he get along well with the girls?" asked Woodford.

"Billy's a flirt and the girls like that. In the beginning it seemed like friendly banter, so I tolerated it. It soon became apparent that his behavior could be construed as sexual harassment. I warned him if there was another instance of verbal or physical affection, like a slap on the butt, I would terminate his contract. That happened just over a month ago. Should I be worried?"

Woodford paused..."Do you think he might be dating one of the members of your track team, like Liz for instance?"

"He'd better not be or I'll have his frickin balls."

"Coach, how would you describe Billy?"

"He's very athletic, good looking, belongs to a couple of clubs. I'd guess him to be around six-three, maybe two ten, two fifteen, somewhere around there. He's blond, medium length hair, and has a couple of tattoos from when he served in the military. I've got his number here if you'd like."

Woodford jotted down the nine-digit number and thanked Coach Ashford for coming in.

Billy, Billy, Billy. . .What have you been up to, you bad little boy?

After visiting the john and doing the mandatory paper work, Woodford left the privacy of his little cubical and reentered the hectic life of his office where he found Detective McCreary going over her latest notes.

"Jane, I need you to interview Lizzie's friends again. Find out everything they know about this Billy. And if they refuse to give up anything, drag their sorry butts in here."

"May I inquire why?"

"Jane, East High's assistant cross-country coach is a Billy Perkins. He's an ex-marine and physically fits our MO of the Duck Creek killer and the Kwik Shop burglar. If he's the Billy that molested Lizzie and then murdered her, he'll wish he never had a pecker."

CHAPTER 27

Tuesday, July 6th, Two days earlier

When Hund returned home he found Bones still on his back, blood oozing from the ragged tear in his buddy's shoulder.

Kneeling, Hund managed to get one hand under each armpit and lift Bone's dead weight onto the kitchen table. He grabbed a dishtowel and tucked it under the head of his dying friend. Bones was out cold.

Hund crossed the kitchen, reached above the new Maytag fridge and turned on the radio to his favorite country-western station, 103.7, where Long Neck Bottle by Garth Brooks was playing. He hummed along as he prepped for the procedure, one he doubted would be successful.

"Well, Bones...here goes nothin." First, Hund rigged a saline drip that would supplant the large quantity of blood lost. Next, he picked a couple of pieces of cloth from the wound, then sterilized the shoulder area.

Lastly, he took a swig of Jack and a deep breath to calm his nerves and dug in, so to speak.

The damage to the artery was substantial, but limited to a single tear. He had worked on much worse in Iraq and Afghanistan.

The whole process took less than an hour. Satisfied, Hund closed the wound before collapsing to the floor with fingers crossed. He watched as Bone's chest rose and fell in a rhythmic motion. Satisfied his patient would survive, he gave into the fifth of Jack calling his name. He told himself just one shot, which turned into another and another until his mouth was numb and the bottle empty. His nose was running and his eyes began to blur, payment in full.

Remnants of the song, Long Neck Bottle, tumbled through his brain as the empty bottle of Jack slipped through his fingers and rattled to the floor.

Thirty minutes later Bones began to stir.

Hund pulled himself up using a leg from the table, stumbled to the sink and plunged his head under a stream of cold water. Using his fingers, he combed his straggly locks to the back of his head, and turned to see Bones sitting on the edge of the table, fingering his bandaged shoulder.

"Man, you's lucky to be alive, that's all I gots ta say. If I were you's, I'd be buying me a lotto ticket. How you feel, bro?"

"Fine...I guess," mumbled a still drowsy Bones.

Hund got him a glass of water and a banana, and then helped him to the recliner.

Through bites of the over ripe fruit and sips of H2O, the two talked about old times, and then Doc made the biggest mistake of his life.

"Bones, I was listening to da radio and they were talking about a murder dis morning. You know anything about that?"

"No, but then I don't listen to the radio much. Hey, can you get me a bottle? I could use a little Jack."

Hund returned to the kitchen and reached deep into the liquor cabinet for a new bottle of Jack Daniels. When he turned back, Bones was standing right behind him. He wore a sinister look, his nose flared, and without warning, Bones plunged the van key deep into Doc's shoulder. "Sorry, Tinker, but the police are looking for a murderer and tag, you're it."

Hund lunged for the towel on the table, but the pressure he applied was too little and too late. His eyes pleaded for help, but Bones just chuckled as Hund crumpled to the floor. The bottle of Jack still grasped tightly in his grip. Bones returned to the recliner, pressed the newly opened bottle of Jack to his lips, and watched Hund die a horrible death.

***

Bones eyes slowly closed, his head nodded to one side, and within minutes fell sound asleep. He woke three hours later, probing at his wound for signs of leakage before heading to the bathroom for a hot shower. He felt pretty good, all things considered. A bit of a headache, but that was to be expected.

Careful not to step in any blood, Bones cleaned up the kitchen, throwing everything into a garbage bag, and sauntered to the door, confident once again that he was the best. He paused as he passed his ex-buddy...and gave Tinker a sharp kick to the ribs.

"Just seeing if you're dead, brother."

As an after-thought, he grabbed Hund's car keys off a hook and went out to the garage to clean up any trace evidence he'd left behind. He toyed with the idea of torching the place, but ditched the idea as too risky. Someone might see the smoke and flames before he made his escape. He replaced the van key, did another once-over, and drove off in Hund's old beater.

CHAPTER 28

Nunavut, Canada, Sawtooth Range

The eight-seater seaplane could be heard coming in from the south, but the five men seated by the roaring fire paid little attention. They didn't even bother to reach for their arsenal of weapons lying at their side.

As the plane glided towards shore, the sounds of hydraulic lifts were heard coming from the water. An unseen forty-foot dock slowly lifted out of the lake and the plane nudged its way toward one of the pylons.

A single man disembarked and with the help of a cane, slowly made his way up the rocky shoreline. It took him twenty minutes to weave his way through the pines to the roaring campfire. As he approached, one man stood, and together the two silently worked their way deeper into the woods.

Built into the nearby limestone cliff was a ten-thousand square foot fortress that could easily accommodate eight men. A unique maze led another thousand feet deeper into the mountain where a three-thousand square foot vault held their tools of the trade and a billion-dollars-plus of stolen booty.

A four-inch thick tungsten steel door guarded the entrance and was designed to blend into the surrounding country side. Once one of the eight fourteen-digit codes were properly entered, the door would slide into the mountain and the hum of a 150KW liquid cooled generator could be heard.

Only one man, a trapper, ever came across the compound. After enjoying a hearty meal, drinks, and a night of jovial conversation, he was never seen again.

The lake only covered a few square miles over part of the vast Canadian wilderness. You couldn't find it on any map, and as far as the men knew it didn't have a name, and they preferred it that way.

The six men who built this fortress, known as the "Hive", were mercenaries. Each man was hand-picked because of his specific skills. The hive was stockpiled with the newest technology in weaponry, and the latest in computer spyware. Other than the six men who were sharing a meal, no one knew of the Hive, including wives, family and friends.

On Friday, July 2nd, five of the men were dropped off for their annual two-week fishing trip. The sixth returned home for some unfinished business. His return tonight gave him an alibi. Not that he'd need one. The brotherhood took care of their own, no matter what the reason or deed that needed to be done.

Twenty minutes later the two men returned and joined in the feast of trout, salmon, wild mushrooms, and red potatoes. They talked about their upcoming raid in Syria and split up their take from their last foray. Each man pocketed a small stipend. The rest, like always, was stored in the vault below for a rainy day.

As the night began to close in, the last hints of the seaplane's engine could be heard as it cleared the mountain range at the end of the lake. The dock slowly slipped back into the clear blue waters, and the door slid closed on their mountain hideaway. All was silent.

CHAPTER 29

Thursday, July 8th

Since the 9-1-1 call last Tuesday, all of the homicide detectives had been pulling extra shifts. Detective Woodford's knuckles were dragging on the floor and he suspected every member of his team was going through pretty much the same thing. There would be no overtime tonight. Everyone needed a break, including him.

Woodford glanced around the office. His team looked hard at work. Jane was bouncing on her red ball as she tried to find a connection between the Kwik shop robberies and their murder case. She must have been onto something, as the bouncing increased the longer she talked on the phone. Or it was a sign of frustration. The snarl, as she hung up, signaled the latter.

Squid sat in an adjoining cubical trying to make contact with Holly Jorgensen of Chicago, the owner of the blue van. After several minutes without saying a word, he finally disconnected and turned toward Woodford. The look on Squid's face was ominous.

"Better take a seat, boss, more bad news.

"On July 4th, a slaying happened in Chicago, a Holly Jorgensen, same MO as Liz Porter and as you know, the owner of the blue van. I've set up a Skype call with Precinct Captain Terri McHayes which should be up and running any second now."

The large screen at the far end of the boardroom cleared of static and they began their one-on-one with McHayes.

"Since this is my dime, I'll begin introductions. I'm Homicide Detective Brian Woodford. My 2nd is Detective Jane McCreary. If at any time I'm not available, she's the one you'll deal with."

One by one the rest of his team stood and were introduced.

McHayes thanked Woodford and shared her introductions.

Little time was wasted before they began discussing the two homicides. Since Holly was murdered first, McHayes led off the discussion.

"Woodford, on July 2nd, we received a 9-1-1 concerning a slaying taking place a mile west of the station. Our squad arrived within minutes, but the man disappeared. The victim was Holly Jorgensen. Someone attacked her, surgically sliced her neck, then stripped off her clothes and raped..."

"Pardon my interruption, but did she get stabbed and have her panties pulled over her head?" inquired Woodford.

"How did you know? That info was never released to the public."

"Same MO as our murder victim, Liz Porter. Did he use a broken tree limb to rape Holly?"

"No, the sawed-off end of a baseball bat."

"Jane, would you like to explain where we stand in our investigation?" asked Woodford.

"Happy to." Jane stood and took her place behind the lectern. "Captain...mind if I call you Terri? I'd feel a lot more comfortable."

Jane continued. "So, Terri. Our two cases have very similar MO's so I'll spare you the details. However, what you may not be aware of is on the same day, moments after our first murder, the killer attacked and tried to silence another girl named Tillie Silvermann. Somehow, Tillie managed to stab our perp with a key, no less, before being tossed into Duck Creek. She narrowly survived by clinging to a tree limb for several hours before being rescued by a local student. It's a fantastic story and one I'd love to share, perhaps another time.

"We also have a second slaying involving our killer. Our two murders are uniquely tied together but totally different MO's. The second involves an adult male, whom we believe was stabbed with a key and died at his home. We believe this man stitched up our perp before being murdered. This has another unbelievable scenario that needs to be shared." Jane stole a quick peek in Woodford's direction, who vigorously shook his head no.

"Fine." Jane stepped away from the podium and Woodford took charge.

"Terri, I believe we're closing in on a possible suspect. Perhaps we could combine our efforts with us taking the lead. If you have no objections, perhaps you could send a detective our way who could assist us and in return share any info and concerns he might have with you?"

"Brian, I have a cracker-jack detective in mind whom I'm sure would love to get out of Chi-town. His name is Frank DeAngelo. But, call him Frankie. He'll be on the first plane out tomorrow morning."

"Why do I get the feeling I'm being duped. Is there something I should be aware of?" queried Woodford.

"Nope, he's a great officer, a strong team player and an all-around fine person."

After a moment's hesitation, Terri flashed a broad smile. "Perhaps I should mention, he's also my brother."

There was much to be discussed and plans needed to be made before they could call it an evening.

All of Brian's team departed for parts unknown, leaving Jane and Woodford to sort out the details.

***

The two detectives left the boardroom to the morning's cleaning crew and exited to the quiet confines of Brian's office.

"Jane, any more leads forthcoming from Hatfield and Ahlstrom?"

"Brian, Sue and Becky are harder to locate than 'Where's Waldo.' Even when I do make contact they clam up. These two are so scared, I doubt if they'll ever come clean.

"I did some digging into Billy's life before we skyped with Chicago. For all intents and purposes, Billy is an average hardworking citizen. His only sin...his first name is Billy and we can't charge him for murder of Liz or label him a pedophile just because his parents couldn't foresee his future.

"I must admit I find it intriguing that Billy fits the profile of our killer and Kwik Shop thief. And he has a close relationship with the track team. I find these coincidences alarming and come tomorrow morning I'll be doing a little one-on-one with Becky and Sue. If they are not forthcoming I'll bring them in and let you take a crack at them."

CHAPTER 30

Thursday, July 8th

Brian checked his watch. It was well past 8:00 and he'd promised to see Amy around 7:00.

On the third ring, Amy answered, "Hello?"

"Hi, Amy. Sorry to call so late, but I've been tied up in the office dealing with another homicide. This one in Chicago, same MO as Lizzie's case. We also have reliable information concerning a Billy Perkins. Does that name raise any alarms?"

"Isn't he a track coach at East? I seem to recall Liz mentioning a Coach Perkins a time or two. Nothing negative, just track related."

"How are you holding up?"

"Ok, I guess. Several of the moms and Coach Ashford stopped by this evening and brought along a tuna casserole. I saved you a large portion. I know it's your favorite."

"I know it's late, but do you still want me to come over? To visit, not to share your tuna, of course."

"Oh, Brian, you make me laugh. It seems like ages since I shared so much as a smile, let alone a laugh with anyone. But, no. It's late and Nana has already retired for the evening. Perhaps tomorrow we could meet for lunch. You choose."

"I'll give it some thought. And Amy, rest assured there'll be security watching your place 24/7. So, try and get a good night's sleep and I'll see you tomorrow." They said their goodbyes and Brian hung up.

Jane heard everything, most everything. "BRIAN!"

Brian spun in his chair and faced a woman with both hands on her hips and a scowl on her face.

"Brian Woodford, on NCIS what is Gibb's rule #10?"

He didn't even have a chance to answer.

"I'll tell you! Never, never become involved with one of your victims. Never! Brian, that poor woman just lost her daughter to a deranged killer and you're inviting her out to lunch!"

"But..."

"No buts. She hasn't even laid her baby girl to rest. I know you two were a thing in the past, but Brian, SHE'S STILL MARRIED! Are you crazy?"

Woodford tried to explain his point of view, but it was a lost cause.

Jane stopped at the door, spun and faced Woodford. "NEVER!"

CHAPTER 31

Class reunion, Circle Tap, Thursday, July 8th

The Skype with Chicago ended and Sergeant Carl "Squid" Hawthorne headed home for a shower and change of clothes. Tonight was the first get-together for his 20th high school reunion. He checked out the yearbook one last time, trying to recall all the names of his high school buddies and old flames, and then gave up.

At 7:30 he arrived at the Circle Tap and found the party well under way. An enclosed outdoor area at the Tap was reserved strictly for his high school reunion. It included a small bar and a self-serving tapper. There were several picnic tables and plenty of standing room. The place could seat a hundred-plus and it was filled to capacity. Carl checked in, filled out a nametag, and went straight to the tapper for a cold Coors Light. He filled a glass and slammed half of it home before heading out to see whom he might remember.

Dan Cain, Roger Timberline, Mary Lou Townsman, and Jackie Petersen, the class reunion officers, were the first to meet and greet. Dan and Roger obviously tapped the keg very early that afternoon and were already slurring words. He wanted to warn them about drunk driving, but why put a damper on the festivities so early in the evening? Jackie came up, grabbed his butt and planted a juicy kiss on his cheek. Obviously, the guys weren't the only ones to hit the booze early.

"Remember me, handsome?"

How could he forget? Jackie was crowned homecoming queen and the best looking, sexiest gal in the class. Now she was lucky if she could stop the scales at 200. Twenty years had done her no favors. Mary Lou, however, looked like she could still fit into her prom dress and didn't look a day over 30.

"Hi, Mary Lou, you look fantastic."

With that, Jackie spun on her heels as if to say, "Screw you," and went off to hit on some other unfortunate guy.

"Thanks, Carl, you look pretty good yourself. Are you here by yourself or with your wife?"

"No, I'm married to my job. Never could find the right girl. Maybe someday."

Just then he got slugged in the arm. He spun around ready for a fight, but instead saw his best friend from East High, Bobby Rangel. They hadn't seen each other since their high school days.

"Carl, it looks like you two have some catching up to do. I see some new faces, so how about later we get together and you can buy a lonely girl a drink." Mary Lou winked and went on her way.

He turned around and slugged Bobby. "They still call you Stinky?"

"Damn it, Carl, keep it down. I haven't heard that moniker since I moved away, and I want to keep it that way. So, do they still call you Squid?"

"Yeah, there's still a few of the old boys around who like to tag me with that. So, let's make a deal, no Stinky and no Squid, okay?"

They shook on it and went off to get another beer and a plate of the best ribs in town.

"So, Bobby, what have you been up to the past twenty years?"

"Thanks to some Apple stock I inherited, I'm retired. I still pick up odd jobs here and there to keep me in pocket change. You know. How about you?"

"Working my way up the ladder at the Davenport PD. Not much else really."

They continued talking of days gone by. Then Bobby saw an old flame he'd like to renew, so he bid his buddy Carl a good night.

There were a lot of faces Carl didn't recognize, but the help of nametags jogged memories of good times at EHS.

After several cold Coors, he was ready for a shot and went inside and pulled up a stool at the far end of the horseshoe-shaped bar. The gal working the counter was hot from the top of her brunette head to the bright red polish on her toes.

The guy sitting next to him gave him a nudge. "That's Michelle! She's the only reason I come here on Thursday nights. That and the cheap beer."

"Hi, I'm Carl. You look familiar. Are you here for the class reunion?"

"Nope. I graduated from West High the same year. I hung out with a lot of East kids during high school so I thought I'd stop and see who I knew, and of course, to check out Michelle. Can I buy you a beer?"

"No, thanks, but I'll buy you a shot if you'd like."

"Tequila's my drink of choice," said Carl's new drinking buddy.

Michelle arrived. "What can I get you, sweetie?"

"Give us a couple of shots of your best tequila, would you darling?" When she turned away to get his order, Carl hit his chest a couple of times and proclaimed he was in lust.

When she returned with the drinks, Carl threw a $20 on the counter.

"Thanks, and keep the change." Both men raised their arms and clanked their glasses, "To Michelle!"

The two chatted, listened to a few tunes, and of course, watched their favorite waitress before Carl excused himself and weaved his way through the packed bar out to the patio.

***

Before the Skype that evening, Woodford advised the team that James might be in town for his class reunion. "Carl, you're heading out to the festivities this evening. Keep an eye out for James and if you see him, bring him in. There's a lot of questions that need to be answered."

Squid checked his yearbook when he got home, and just for the hell of it, looked up Ricky as well. There were several team shots of the two, but the spaces reserved for senior pictures were bare. "Strange."

It was closing in on 10:00 when Carl worked his way back to Mary Lou. He took her hand and guided her into the bar where they found a quiet corner, or at least as quiet as it gets on college night. Michelle became a distant memory.

They had a quiet conversation going when a loud drunk yelled, "Mary Lou, remember me?"

Carl turned and came face to face with James Porter. At least that's what it said on his nametag.

"Porter, I need to talk to you!"

James gave him a sucker punch to the face, then a kick to the balls, and Squid dropped like the thermometer on a wind chilled winter day. Porter ran out the door, past the smokers, and headed up the alley before Hawthorne could get off the floor.

It was all he could do to pull out his wallet and show his badge. "Someone call 9-1-1! Get the cops here now!"

Mary Lou crouched in the corner crying. "I hated that creep when we were in high school and I hate him even more now."

Carl crawled closer and took her hand. "I'm okay, just a little blood and some really sore...you know."

A few minutes later Carl spotted Woodford as he entered the bar and guided Mary Lou through the crowd to meet his boss.

"Mary Lou, this is the great Detective Brian Woodford I've been telling you about."

"Nice to meet you, Detective."

"The pleasure's all mine. Carl, I just heard a 10-10 call come through about a fight, officer down. You somehow involved?"

"Yeah, I tried questioning James Porter, but the bastard

sucker punched me. I never stood a chance."

"Carl, did you or Mary Lou get a good look at Porter?"

"Sure, why?"

"Did either of you notice if Porter displayed an injury to his neck or shoulder?"

Carl admitted he never got a look before being knocked to the floor.

"Detective, I'm not sure what you mean," Mary Lou said.

"Did he have a Band-Aid or something wrapped around his neck or shoulder? Something that could possibly hide a wound?"

"I don't think so, but it happened so fast. All I remember is Porter's face."

"That's okay. Why don't the two of you join the rest of your friends and Carl, I'll see you tomorrow morning."

Woodford started to walk away and then turned, "A lot has happened since we last talked, so get in early."

Brian spent the next hour watching videos from the bar's three security cameras and was rewarded with several full frontals of James. He downloaded the videos, finished the last of his beer, and tipped the barmaid. He spent the next twenty minutes driving the streets of Davenport. His every thought focused on James Porter and how he would bring him to justice.

CHAPTER 32

Thursday, July 8th/9th

Mary Lou rolled over in bed, braced herself on one elbow and studied the unshaven face of Sergeant Carl Squid Hawthorne.

"You feeling any better, Sergeant?"

"Much better now, thanks to you."

"I didn't hurt you, did I?"

Carl softly put a finger to her lips.

"Shhhhh."

He raised his hand and carefully combed his fingers through her hair.

"What color are your eyes? They're beautiful."

She smiled. "My dad used to say, 'They're as deep and blue as any ocean he'd ever sailed, and someday, a man's going to come along and drown in them if he's not careful.' You going to drown in them, sailor?"

He was being drawn deeper and deeper into her eyes and her luscious smile. He couldn't stop himself, and if truth be told, he didn't want to.

Their fingers intertwined as their eye-lids drooped and they slid off together into a deep and wonderful sleep.

As the morning rays filtered through the eastern blinds, Carl rolled over to an empty bed. A crushing disappointment overcame him until he smelled coffee brewing in the kitchen.

It was going to be a beautiful day.

CHAPTER 33

Friday, July 9th

After arriving at headquarters, Woodford called CSI Tom Perdan and Trent Buckley into his office. "I've got a new assignment for you, Tom, and I think you're going to love this one. James Porter was at the Circle Tap last night, and we have full frontal video of him attacking Hawthorne. Tom, go over the images and see if there are any flesh wounds or bandages on his neck. He's got what looks to be at least a six-day growth. Fine-toothed comb. Got it?"

"Trent, I need an APB out as soon as possible. If we can't nail him for the murder of Liz Porter, we sure as hell can put him behind bars for assaulting one of my officers."

***

Carl floated into the office just before 9:00. Frank DeAngelo arrived from Chicago fifteen minutes later. Introductions were made and over the next hour the two murder cases were covered in minute detail.

The team decided that McCreary and DeAngelo would focus on Billy Perkins. Hawthorne and Woodford would take on James and Ricky Porter.

Hawthorne was nearly giddy that he got to work with Woodford instead of McCreary. *Detective badge, here I come.*

CHAPTER 34

Friday, July 9th

After the three Kwik shop robberies, he'd acquired enough money for a day at the casino where he could make some real bread. He liked blackjack, but loved craps. He decided to head to Jumer's in Rock Island for two reasons. It was the newest casino in the Quad Cities, and he hadn't robbed any stores on that side of the river.

There was a lot of action on the craps table, and from the sounds of the crowd everything was going their way.

"Nine, nine, winner every time!" came the call, and the players began raking in their chips. "Place your bets, folks. Is everyone off the hard ways? I've got a $5 world, and the dice are out. It's a 7, winner, winner, chicken dinner, pay the line!"

There wasn't a spot open for him to squeeze into. He watched for another ten minutes but couldn't stand it. Some people enjoyed all the luck. Maybe his would be at the blackjack table.

He walked over to where the table games were being played and found an empty $25 to $500 blackjack table with a pretty little blond shuffling the cards. He pulled out a wad of $100 bills and asked for all black. He liked playing two hands, so he placed two $200 bets. His first hand was 19, and he stayed. His second hand showed a pair of aces. He put another $200 down and split. The dealer hit the first ace with a nine for twenty and the second ace with a four for fifteen. He was feeling pretty good right now. The sweet little blond turned her bottom card, which showed a five, giving her eleven. The next card out of the shoe was a face card. Twenty-one.

He just lost $600 and he'd only played a minute. "Oh, hell, easy-come, easy go."

Things got better for a while. He hit a couple of blackjacks and the dealer broke three straight. He increased his bets to $400 a hand and won both, gave the blond a wink of thanks, and tossed her a black chip. This was going to be his day.

The bar maid came by and he ordered a Jack Daniels on the rocks and settled in for what he hoped would be a long day of winning.

An hour later all he had left was one green, $25 chip. His pockets were empty and he already hit the ATM machine twice. The craps table was now wide open. He chose a spot and placed his $25 chip on the line.

"Welcome to Jumer's and good luck," came the call.

Johnny, the stick man, pushed all six red dice in front of the new player, and waited till the roller chose two.

Of the six dice, there were two 5's, a 6, and three 3's, his favorite number. He picked up two of the 3's with his thumb and pointer finger and lightly blew on them for good luck and then tossed them down the length of the table. A pair of 6's. He crapped out on his first roll.

"This place sucks!" he screamed at the top of his lungs.

He grabbed the rest of his drink, slammed down the last finger of whiskey and threw the plastic cup towards a waste bin.

"Air ball!" called the pit boss, which is all he heard as he adjusted his Yankee's ball cap and walked out into the sunshine. His truck was parked halfway across the lot and with each step the string of cuss words became a little louder, until he jumped into the cab, threw it into first and fishtailed out of the parking lot and onto the interstate.

CHAPTER 35

Friday, July 9th

When the team arrived back from their break, Jane began updating the white board while Woodford, DeAngelo and Hawthorne worked the computers.

After two hours of futility it became apparent the Porter cousins were enigmas. It was like someone took a magic eraser and wiped their life history off the face of the earth.

The DMV displayed no record of James ever having a driver's license. No credit cards, no phones, nor ever having paid income taxes, state or federal. According to Amy Porter, James served in Special Forces, but no records existed of him serving in any branch of the service.

Ricky married Amy right out of college. But their search revealed nothing of his life. No marriage certificate, no work or military history, zip, zero. Like James, his life was erased from every data base they searched. Follow the money trail, except, no trail could be found. No record of him ever working. So where did he get his money?

Detectives Harold Steinman and Charlie Owens were sent back to re-interview Patty Sue Porter, Ricky's second wife. They were given explicit instructions to find out everything they could about Ricky and Patty Sue's history together. If she refused to cooperate they were to bring her in.

Someone suggested the Porters could be in witness protection. Which might make sense if they were shipped off to some desolate area in Wyoming and their names were changed. But Ricky and James were still using their given names, and Ricky still lived in Davenport, or did he? Perhaps when Detectives Steinman and Owens returned they might be able to fill in some blanks.

Carl suggested CIA or Russian moles. All ideas were entertained, even if some bordered on bizarre.

Ricky Porter...Carl couldn't shake the name from his subconscious. He thought for sure he knew a Ricky Porter from High School. He'd checked his yearbook the night before and there was no Rick or Ricky Porter in his senior class. Then it struck him like a bolt of lightning.

Carl slammed his fist into the desk. "Damn it. I knew I recognized that face. Last night at the Circle I bought a man a shot. It was Ricky Porter, I'm sure of it! He got kicked out of East High for fighting. I think he took a knife to some kid."

Carl put in a call to juvie and asked for a search for anything on a Ricky Porter. Minutes later a call came back. Nothing. Another dead end.

"You're a regular Porter magnet," said DeAngelo. "You buy one a drink and get kicked in the nads by the other. At least we know they're both in town." DeAngelo continued, "I'm going to check the Porter family tree and see if any other Porters might be housing our cousins."

Woodford checked the clock. It was closing in on noon and he planned to meet Amy for lunch. Hopefully she could put a new spin on her ex-husbands.

He adjourned the meeting and told everyone to be back in the conference room by 2:00.

Jane gave him a shake of the head and mouthed the words... "Rule #10...NEVER."

Jane and Frankie made their way to the Filling Station for wings. Later they'd visit the hospital so Frankie could meet Tillie. Carl went straight to his desk and called Mary Lou.

CHAPTER 36

Friday, July 9th

Amy sat waiting on the porch for Woodford when he arrived. He ascended the steps and accepted the seat next to her on the swing.

The dark rings under her eyes were all but gone and she exhibited some color in her cheeks. She smiled as Brian sat down and took her hand.

"Brian, can we do lunch first? My appetite has returned and I'm feeling a bit lightheaded. Then, perhaps, you'll tell me what took place in Chicago."

They chose Panera's for their famous soups and sandwiches.

They arrived just after twelve-thirty and, as usual, the parking lot was packed. The line moved quickly, however, and when it came time to place their orders, Amy chose the "Pick Two" with a tuna on rye, a cup of chicken noodle soup, and a large raspberry iced tea.

Yes, this could be a woman he would change his life for.

"I'll take the same," said Woodford.

They waited off to one side and took full advantage of all the free smells Panera's offered. Eventually their names were called and Woodford grabbed the tray. Together they went in search of a quiet place to enjoy their meal and share a moment together. A young couple carrying a small baby with a Dairy Queen twist to its red hair was just leaving their table as Brian and Amy took their lunch out onto the patio. The small table, with its mosaic inserts, sat apart from the others, leaving Brian and Amy the luxury of a quiet space to converse.

Brian lowered his head, and as promised, quietly told of the execution style murder of Holly Jorgensen, but spared Amy the grizzly details. Aspects of the attack on Hawthorne shook Amy to her very core. So, too, did the information she was about to share with Brian.

"James called. Last night he attended his class reunion where someone offered condolences on the death of his daughter. He told me he'd been out of town on business and hadn't heard. Then he had the gall to say, 'Now that Liz is dead, would you like to get back together again?' I was speechless and slammed the phone down. Brian, if he ever comes near me I'll kill him! I'm sorry. I shouldn't have said that, but he just...just...makes me so, so angry! I can't help myself."

Brian changed the subject to what they'd found out about the cousins, or lack thereof.

Amy was speechless. Stunned would be a better word. All those years she'd never known what was going on behind her back. Nana warned her the Porters were nothing but trouble, but she'd listened with her heart, not her mind. That is until James did the unthinkable and slapped Liz.

Brian gently quizzed her about old drinking buddies or relatives that might take in James or Ricky, but none came to mind. *Enough is enough.* He'd ruined their lunch. It was time to repair the moment and get on with it.

It had been a quick two hours and the time had come to head back to the station. After dropping Amy off, he checked his mirrors. A rusted-out Honda was parked just down the street, and the driver's head peeked out from above the steering wheel. He thought it may have been tailing him since the restaurant, and now he was sure of it. Hund owned an old Honda Accord, and this car matched its description.

As he swung out to give chase, two kids on skateboards blocked his path. He laid on the horn, but the kids flipped him the bird and flashed shit eating grins as they slowly rolled down the center of the road. All he could do was watch as the dark green car made a quick right turn and disappeared from sight.

Lizzie's killer drove that car. He'd bet his pension on it. He radioed the station, put out an APB, and requested a backup. The Porter's house was going to have 24-7 surveillance, no matter the cost, even if it meant paying for it out of his own pocket.

Woodford circled the block a couple of times, then pulled to the curb and called Amy Porter.

"Amy, it's Brian. Would you like some company this evening? I could bring a pizza over."

"I'd love company, but not the pizza. There's still tuna casserole left over from last night. Care to share?"

CHAPTER 37

Friday, July 9th

The wings at the Filling Station took thirty minutes to prepare, which offered DeAngelo and McCreary a chance to connect. Their career paths took much the same course, early success leading to early advancement. Frankie was married with twin girls, and like Jane, was married to his job and happy, for the most part. The wings arrived, his hot and spicy, hers covered in a Blue Cheese concoction for which the Station was renowned.

After much finger licking and a third refill of iced tea, the duo made their way to Genesis East. First stop, the morgue, where Jane introduced DeAngelo to Dr. Ball. Insights were shared, as were the left over hot wings. Next up, a visit to the third floor and Tillie Silvermann.

Tillie was awake and managing to eat some chocolate ice cream with sprinkles when the detectives entered her room.

"Good afternoon, Tillie. Remember me?"

"Hi, Jane. Got some good news today. Doc says I should be up and running in no time."

"Girl, you are amazing. If you make it to the Bix, I'll personally be there to cheer you on."

"Jane, who's your good-looking friend?" asked Tillie with a sheepish grin.

"Tillie, this is Detective Frank DeAngelo. He's from Chicago. They have a case similar to Liz Porter's and he's here to assist."

"Hi, Tillie. Call me Frankie. Jane told me about your ordeal. I must say your recovery is nothing short of miraculous."

This brought a smile to her face that caused her to cringe, just a little.

"Sorry. Jane tells me you're having trouble remembering the attack. Is that true?"

"Yeah. It's so frustrating. I can picture him coming at me, and I see his face, his hands, and blood. Then I wake up and he's gone...nothing. I want to help but I just can't remember."

They talked a little longer, but Tillie was beginning to tire and DeAngelo and McCreary needed to return to the station.

Jane was tempted to show Tillie the image they retrieved from the Circle Tap video, but dashed that thought until she talked with Dr. Oberhaus. She didn't want to short change Tillie's memory any more than it already was.

As they exited, Dusty Anders, Tillie's savior, came into the room with a big bouquet of flowers and a teddy bear.

"Hi, Dusty," said Jane. She turned towards Tillie and gave her a little wink. Tillie smiled and winked back.

CHAPTER 38

Friday, July 9th

It was close to 3:00 by the time the whole team returned to the office. The shocking news of the hour came when Detectives Steinman and Owens returned from the interview, or lack of it, with Patty Sue Porter. The house had been stripped. The search yielded not so much as a day-old newspaper. They dusted for prints. Nada. The place appeared to have been professionally sanitized.

They spent the last three hours quizzing neighbors, but no one saw or heard a thing.

The APB for the Honda Accord yielded nothing. They held a stakeout at Billy Perkins's apartment but no one went in or out the whole day.

By 5:30 Brian decided to call it quits for the evening.

Woodford headed home to feed Barker and take him for a walk. Later, he would spend the evening with Amy. Jane and DeAngelo agreed to work the stakeout of Billy Perkins' apartment. Jane wanted a piece of that action and wasn't about to let him slip through her fingers.

***

Squid checked his watch and decided he could grab a quick shower and shave before making it over to the golf course to surprise Mary Lou.

It had been a tough week. Everyone put in a ton of over-time, so Brian gave them the weekend off, with instructions to stay close to their phones in case something new materialized. With any luck, they'd all come back fresh on Monday and put an end to this case. He could dream, couldn't he? Or was that not allowed?

That holy dream-that holy dream,
While all the world was chiding,
Hath cheered me as a lovely beam
A lonely spirit guiding.

Edgar Allen Poe

CHAPTER 39

Friday, July 9th

Eight thousand dollars! How could he have blown that much money in one day? He had bills to pay, one in particular.

He drove around town all afternoon, debating on which Kwik Shop to strike next. He hated the franchise ever since he'd been ripped out of a paycheck back in his teens. He'd been lucky. Well, not really. Luck had nothing to do with it. Over the past few months he staked out all the Kwik Shops in town and knew which cash registers were ripe for plucking. He planned this for weeks and then he blew his whole wad at the casino.

A Kwik Shop near 53rd and Welcome Way was going to be his honey hole, his last job. The store did a thriving business, but there were always two employees manning the counter. Not so this evening. Good news for him. But what stood between him and his payday was a middle-aged black woman who looked like she could tear him a new one.

He patted his hip pocket. His six-inch serrated service blade was secure and out of sight. The last customer left with a twelve pack of Pepsi. It was now or never. He put down his binoculars and pulled his hat over his eyes and casually crossed the street.

He crashed through the door, scattering a display of candy snacks. He didn't hesitate. He bounded over the counter and grabbed her by the hair, yanking her upwards. The security alarm was shrilling out a warning.

How much time did he have? He didn't know, but he wasn't going to leave without the money.

"Hand over the cash, darling, and you won't get hurt!"

"Don't call me darling! You ain't my old man."

"Shut up and give me the cash."

"Screw you! You ain't getting nothing except the back of my hand."

The tip of his knife pressed against her neck and droplets of blood trickled down the blade, staining her ivory work shirt.

She grabbed a brown paper bag and began filling it with ones, fives and tens.

"Just the big bills and hurry!

"COME ON...COME ON!" he screamed over the wailing of the alarm.

He twisted his head towards the display window. "Shit!" He could see a car pulling into the drive.

He watched as she finished with the tens and twenties and handed him the sack.

"Lift up the drawer, damn it, and hurry!"

He was beginning to panic. He'd already spent way too much time in the store and now a customer was about to enter.

Tick...Tock...Tick...Tock

The drawer held at least two-thousand in large bills, and as she dropped the Grants and Franklins into the sack the bell above the door rang an ominous tone.

"Police! Drop the knife and lift your hands so I can see them!"

"Shit!" he screamed.

Ducking behind the clerk, he reapplied pressure, forcing the blade to slice deeper into her neck.

"Lady, do everything I say and you won't get hurt."

As the blade dug in, he slowly backed his way to the storage room door.

"Don't be stupid, son! There's no way out!"

He butted his way into the storage room and pointed his knife at the cop. "Screw with me, and she dies."

He slammed the door shut and rammed the dead bolt home. Turning, he slapped the woman, knocking her to the floor. "It's all your fault. All you had to do was give me the money. But, no, you wanted to be a frickin hero."

He grabbed the gal's dreadlocks and dragged her to a corner. "Sit down and shut up, and maybe, just maybe, we both might come out of this alive!"

He was pacing the floor like a caged animal when a deep voice called from the outer room.

"Open the door and step out! We have the place surrounded!"

He heard him but was in no hurry to give up just yet.

"I want to talk to your captain. Get him here before I start carving up my lady friend!"

There were two dead bolts on the rear door and no windows. The room held enough food and liquor to keep him satisfied for months. No, there was no hurry to give up just yet. He needed to think.

***

Woodford finished splashing Brut on his face just as his phone rang. He checked his watch. It couldn't be Amy. He wasn't that late.

"Woodford here."

"Woodford, it's Trent. There's a 2-11, robbery in progress, at the Kwik Shop on 53rd and Welcome Way. You want to take this one?"

"What're we looking at?" asked Woodford.

"It's a hostage situation and blood's been spilled. He's holed up in the storage room and threatening to kill a Tamika Gaines, the day shift clerk."

"This clown got a name?" asked Woodford.

"Nope. It just went down."

"Yeah. I got it. Call McCreary and Hawthorne and have them meet me there. I'm about fifteen minutes out. Don't let anybody do anything stupid until I arrive."

He called Amy and apologized, once again, for not being able to make it over. He promised to find a way to make it up to her.

***

Nearly an hour passed since he'd taken his hostage and locked himself into the storage room. He'd finished off a six-pack of warm beer and a dozen Slim Jims when three knocks came on the door.

Woodford's deep baritone voice bellowed through the cracks.

"My name's Captain Woodford." A little white lie, but if the man wanted to talk to the Captain, then Captain he would be.

"What's your name?" asked Woodford.

Silence.

"Come on, give me a name so I know what to call you."

After what seemed like an eternity a voice called out, "Chuck. You know, like woodchuck. How much wood could a woodchuck chuck if a woodchuck could chuck wood," came the reply.

"Funny, I like that. It shows you have a sense of humor," said Woodford. "But there's nothing funny about the situation you're in. You're looking at twenty with no parole, minimum. Is that something you can laugh about?"

There was no laughter on either side of the door.

Someone tapped on Woodford's shoulder. It was McCreary and DeAngelo. "Got your back, boss."

Woodford continued, "See, if you give a little, we give a little. That's how this is going to work, ok? So, tell me, Chuck, is our hostage still alive?"

"I'll give you this one, Woodford. She's alive, but if I don't get what I want I'll cut her up and send her out in pieces."

"So, Chuck, if it is Chuck. What is it you want?"

"I've been thinking about that. Let me chuck some more wood and I'll get back to you."

Twenty minutes later Woodchuck was ready to negotiate.

"Captain Woodford, you ready to play a little game?"

"Sorry, Chuck. This is no time for games. What is it you want?"

"Really, Captain? From where I stand I hold all the cards. So, it's time to play Let's Make a Deal."

"Don't like the game, never did," said Woodford.

"Captain, please...hear me out. You're going to love it. In this portion of our game you get to choose what's behind door number one. My lady friend here stays alive and all in one piece if, and only if, you get me a plane with safe passage to the destination of my choice. From there I'll disappear into the night and you'll never see or hear from this Woodchuck ever again.

"Now, if you don't like door number one, you could choose number two, where you'll receive a few small packages. Ten to be exact, one every half-hour until I get my plane and I'm safely out of here. And trust me those little piggies will not be going to market.

"And now we come to door number three. Behind number three is...a dead woman, and I'll probably end up alongside her.

See, I'm not going to prison. So, Captain, pick a door. You have ten minutes to choose. Clock starts...now."

And then he started singing, "How much wood could a woodchuck chuck if a woodchuck could chuck wood? A woodchuck would chuck all the wood he could chuck if a woodchuck could chuck wood," and he started all over again.

Jane looked at Frankie. "If you ask me he's already planning his insanity plea."

Woodford used his ten minutes to chase down Detective Arnold of the Swat team and plan a strategy, one where no one lost their lives or their piggies.

"Captain, you have one minute. This little piggy went to market, this little piggy stayed home, this little piggy gets roast beef, this little piggy gets none, and this little piggy goes wee, wee, wee all the way home. Captain,

I've counted, and she has all ten of her little piggies. At least for now. If you want to keep it that way, you need to make a decision! What's it going to be, Captain? Door number one, two, or three? Thirty seconds."

Detective Arnold grabbed Woodford by the shoulders. "Stall, Brian. Tell him anything, but stall."

"Woodchuck, it's Woodford. It's time to play your game. We'll go with door number one. What is it you want?"

CHAPTER 40

Friday, July 9th

He'd watched the Porter house for several days, long before he killed Lizzie.

Sometimes he would drive by, and other times he would hide behind the bushes in the neighbor's yard and watch, biding his time until he could take out Amy Porter and her mom. There was still an hour before total darkness, so he would just sit and wait. Waiting was an art form, and he was the master.

Reaching deep into his right pocket, he pulled out his "Bones", a pair of ivory dice. He'd owned this particular pair since high school. *Dice was his game and Bones was his name.* The soothing clicks the dice made as he rolled them through his fingers gave him a sense of power, total infallibility. Patiently he waited, occasionally sneaking a furtive glance at the empty street, then casting the dice to the ground over and over.

Darkness closed in and he got ready to move when he heard someone coming up behind him. He sat there, not breathing, not moving a muscle. Maybe they wouldn't see him or maybe it was already too late.

The dog sniffed his crotch, then the bushes, then lifted his leg, peed, and walked off as silently as he had entered. Bones toyed with the idea of killing the damn mutt, but this was its turf, not his. It would live to pee another day.

A lone cloud swallowed up the crescent mid-July moon, casting a pallor over the Porter's neighborhood. He chose this night for just that reason. Just one more thing to do. Roll the bones for good luck.

Snake eyes! The curse of the "Eye" was upon him. Why did he do it? Why did he throw the dice that last time? *Stupid...stupid... stupid.* He was cursed, the dice never lied. Now what should he do? He was so close to enacting his revenge and now the curse of the "Eye".

He sat for what seemed like forever but finally decided, to hell with the dice.

He pushed himself away from the bush and slowly crept across the street. A single beam of moonlight sliced through the cloud striking him in the face. He cursed his dice once more before stepping onto the porch.

The lights of a car two houses down came on and the horn blared as a man jumped out of the driver's side door.

"Police! Step away from the house."

Bones spun towards the voice, dropped, and crabbed walked to the far railing. Reaching up, he grabbed the wooden rail, pushed off with his right leg and landed softly in the flowerbed below. He chanced a quick glance at the chubby officer giving chase, stood and bolted for the alley.

He questioned his skills, his cunning, his invincibility, but in the end Bones knew it was not he that screwed up, it was the "Evil Eye." The dice, the snake eyes, that stupid roll of the die that caused his failure. He reached into his pocket and wrapped his sweaty palm around the cool cubes of ivory. His friends, his only true friends, rattled between his fingers and once again calmed his fears. The cop was nowhere in sight, the sounds of sirens fading with each step. He relaxed his grip and the dice slid back into the recesses of his pocket and his mind.

***

The Rhythm City Casino floated elegantly on the shores of the Mississippi. Its bright lights, 60's tunes, and cheers from late night revelers reflected off the muddy waters and wafted down the river. Bones thought about going in and playing craps, but that would be pushing his luck to the limit.

In the parking lot he removed the plates from a Cadillac Seville and switched them with those from a Mitsubishi Eclipse. If his luck held he'd be out of Dodge before the sheriff in town knew he was even gone. He hotwired the Seville and left the parking lot. His work was not done, not by a long shot. Failure was not in his vocabulary.

CHAPTER 41

Friday, July 9th

Woodchuck wasn't nervous. Hell, he was drunk out of his frickin gourd. He hadn't experienced a buzz like this since his college days.

No, he wasn't worried about the cops or jail. He was worried about the man who helped him out of a jam for a mere ten grand. And he'd already blown eight of it and now, here he was drinking warm beer, eating Slim Jims, and pretending he was a woodchuck. *God, life sucked.*

Woodchuck grabbed another can of Bud Light and a handful of beef jerky and returned to the box of canned Spaghetti O's he'd been sitting on. "Hey, lady, you want a beer?"

Tamika, sitting in the far corner, let out a string of cuss words that would make a preacher blush.

"Your loss. Personally, I'd hate to die and not have a good buzz on."

He was shitfaced drunk and didn't care. He'd slice his own throat, but didn't have the balls to do it. Maybe the girl would do it for him?

Between bites of Jerky and swigs of beer he called to Woodford. His words were slurred as he told what he wanted: "I want a car, a fast one, a private jet, and a couple of hundred grand, no make it three. And if you shoot me, don't hit the face. You'll mess up my fur." He cackled and foam shot out his nose.

He laughed again and started singing little piggies.

"Anything else?" Woodford asked.

Silence.

His beer slipped from his fingers, but he didn't care, he'd just get another. His arms began moving as if he was directing an orchestra, wide sweeping motions going faster and faster as he tried to remember the words to his songs. He began to sing, "Piggy, piggy, woodchuck," and laughed. Then cried.

***

Brian paid little attention to this latest outburst from Woodchuck. He'd just been told that someone tried to break into the Porter household. "Dammit, I was supposed to be there," he said to no one in particular. "I promised."

Jane tapped him on the shoulder and handed him a cup of coffee. "It's all right. I just got off the phone with Amy and she's doing fine."

"Piggy, piggy, time to go to market," came the voice from behind the door.

Things were not going to be fine as long as he stood on this side of the door and Woodchuck and his hostage on the other.

***

Tamika Gaines had never been afraid of nobody and this woodchuck fellow was not going to be the first.

Over the last hour, Tamika sat waiting, watching, and planning as the woodchuck got drunk, then drunker, and more careless by the minute. The time had come to bring her plan to fruition.

"Hey, Mr. Woodchuck, I got'ta pee really bad."

"Ain't no place to pee in here, Miss Piggy."

"Look, I can use that bucket over there, if you promise not to look."

"Go for it, bitch, but don't stink up the place," and his head sagged to his chest.

There was no way she wanted door number two or three. Come to think of it, she didn't particularly care for door number one either.

"Hey, lady, shit or get off the pot." He let out a deep, guttural belly laugh.

That did it. She didn't take that crap from nobody!

"I'm done, Mr. Woodchuck. Mind looking the other way?"

She quickly pulled up her panties and skirt and waited for her chance.

Woodchuck placed his knife on the floor and was struggling to open a Bud Light, when Tamika struck.

She launched the pail of piss into his face and slammed the bucket over his head before grabbing the knife off the floor.

"Now we'll see whose piggies are going to go wee, wee, wee, all the way home!" She laughed at her own joke.

"What's going on in there? You okay, Ms. Gaines?"

"Yeah, I'm fine. I'm teaching Mr. Woodchuck here a lesson on how to treat a lady!"

She slammed the butt of the knife onto the bottom of the bucket. "You keep that on your head, you hear?"

She walked over to the door and undid the latch, opening it for Woodford and the SWAT team.

She handed the knife to Woodford and made a bee-line to the lady's room. She had some serious cleaning up to do.

Woodford rapped the top of the bucket. "You going to behave, Mr. Woodchuck, or do we need to leave that on until we get to the station?"

A drunken, "Yeah," came from beneath the yellow plastic bucket.

Jane read him his rights.

Jane turned to Woodford. "I'll let one of the officers drive him to the station. No way I want my car to smell like this rodent."

As they hauled Woodchuck off in cuffs, Woodford looked at his team and shrugged. "Tonight will go down as one of the weirdest arrests I've ever been associated with. Woodchuck...definitely one for the books."

CHAPTER 42

Friday, July 9th

After Hawthorne took Woodchuck's paw prints and mug-shots, he ran him through a shower. He then escorted him to Interrogation Room A and cuffed him to the table. Fifteen minutes later McCreary and Woodford walked into the room.

"I want to see my lawyer!"

"Well, Mr. Woodchuck, that's your right. Do you have an attorney or does the city of Davenport need to provide one?"

"I'll take a court appointed lawyer," he said with a snarl.

"Do you have a real name, or should I just call you Chuck?"

"Just get me a lawyer, pig!"

"Now, Chuck, you've just upset Detective Woodford and messed up his whole weekend. Why don't you be a nice woodchuck and give us your name?" Jane asked.

"Screw you, lady. I'm not talking until...wait, what the hell? Woodford, you said you were the Captain!"

"A little white lie, Woodchuck. Compared to what you've said and done I think I'm allowed a lie or two."

"Oh, God. I'm going to be sick," bemoaned Woodchuck.

There was a knock on the door. Hawthorne entered and handed Woodford a manila folder.

Woodford opened the folder and did a quick look through. "Well, well, well...Jane, look who we've got here. It's our friendly track coach from Davenport East, Billy Perkins."

All the bluster went out of his sails. "Now, will you get me a lawyer?" asked Perkins.

"You're going to need one, Billy," snarled Woodford. "Sergeant Hawthorne, I want you to add rape and murder to the assault and robbery charges."

"Glad to oblige boss. Anything else you need tonight before we put our woodchuck to bed?"

"That should do it." Woodford and Jane stood up to go.

"Wait a minute, I didn't kill anyone! You can't charge me with murder. It was a lousy robbery!"

"Oh, but we can and we will. So, tell that to your lawyer." Jane looked at the folder. "She should be here sometime early tomorrow."

"No, wait! I don't need a lawyer. You've got me on the burglary stuff, ok. But I ain't no murderer!"

Woodford returned to his chair.

"So, Mr. Perkins, do you wish to revoke your rights to a lawyer until further notice?"

"I do," and he slumped back into his chair. Spittle ran down his chin and tears down his cheeks. And from the smell, there was also leakage below his belt.

Jane pulled out a form from the clipboard she'd been holding and tossed a refusal form and pen onto the table.

"Sign where you see the X."

Woodford turned on the recorder. "Are you ready to make a statement? And just for the record, have you revoked your right to a lawyer?"

Perkins nodded.

"You need to answer all my questions with a verbal response. There will be no nodding of the head."

"Yeah, I don't need a lawyer. I didn't kill anyone. So, let's get this over with."

Woodford began the questioning. "As of right now we're more interested in our murder case than your act of stupidity at the Kwik Shop. Would you tell us where you were last Tuesday morning between 5:30 and 6:00?"

"I don't remember, probably at home in bed."

"Do you sleep alone or did you have company?"

"Sometimes I'll have a lady friend over, but usually I sleep alone."

"Did you have company last Tuesday morning?"

"I don't remember. It was a long 4th of July weekend and I don't remember much of anything from back then."

"Okay, we'll get back to that later. Where were you on the 4th of July?"

"Visiting a friend in Chicago."

"Interesting. Can you give us the name of your friend, for verification?"

"Yeah, sure." Woodchuck provided the essentials: his buddy's name, phone number and address.

Jane looked over at the mirror and motioned for Hawthorne to come in. "Check this guy out and see if Woodchuck's telling the truth."

Woodford started up again. "Billy, I need a timeline from when you left Davenport until your return."

"Damn it, I can't remember what I had for lunch, let alone what I did a week ago." Still, he reached up with cuffed hands and covered his face. For a couple of minutes, he said nothing. "Let's see...I left Davenport Saturday morning around 10:00, no, make that 11:00. I got to Butch's place sometime around 3:00. We sat around for a while and talked a little golf. Then we went to the ballpark for a Cubs game. Afterwards, we stopped in at one of the local bars. I don't remember the name, but Butch will. We chatted up some strippers, drank a couple of buckets of beer, and got home as the sun was coming up."

"Did the girls come back with you to Butch's place?"

He shook his head. "No. I'm sorry. I really don't remember. I know they weren't there when I came to Sunday afternoon."

"Did you do anything special on Sunday?"

"Yeah, we put up some shelves in his garage and cleaned up his work room. I left around 5:30 and once I got home I crashed big time."

It felt like needles were jabbing both eyes and menacing creatures were eating away at his brain. He'd never drink another beer again.

Woodford took a different approach.

"Tell me, Billy, do you think high school girls are hot?"

"What's that got to do with anything?"

"We've been told you like to flirt with the girls on the track team. Is that true?"

"Who the hell told you that?"

"It doesn't matter. Do you think they're hot?"

"Yeah, I suppose...they're young and good looking, you know."

"No, I don't know. You tell me," said Jane.

"Look, lady, I'm human, and when the girls are running and bouncing all over the place, I look. But that's all."

"Do you know Liz Porter?" asked Woodford.

"Sure, Liz is on the track team. She's the one that got wacked, right? Is that what this is all about?"

"Yeah, Billy, that's what this is all about. We talked to a friend of hers who told us Liz was molested by an older guy named Billy. Would you be that Billy?"

"I think I want my lawyer now."

"Good idea," said Woodford. "Good idea."

Billy dropped his head which smacked against the steel table top. His whole body began to shake uncontrollably to the point Woodford was ready to call for EMT's.

As Brian and Jane exited the interrogation room they were met by Squid. "Boss, I don't want to put a damper on your celebration, but when I booked Billy I didn't see any indications of a wound in or around his neck. If he was Lizzie's assailant, he wasn't stabbed."

"Carl, Jane and I have a theory we've been toying with. It's still in its infancy and we'll share it with the team tomorrow. So, until then, everyone enjoy the rest of your evening and we'll see you bright and early tomorrow morning."

***

After three rings, a shallow voice answered, "Hello."

"Amy. It's Brian. We just finished up here at the office and I wanted to check to see if it's still okay to stop over this evening."

"Oh, Brian. I know it's late, but I could really use a shoulder to cry on. Besides, Jane told me all about Woodchuck and I'd be amiss if I said I didn't want to hear about his antics."

"This may sound strange, but, would you mind if I bring my best friend over? I'd like you to meet him."

"I suppose...if you really want to."

"Thanks. He's quite the character. One other thing, do you like Whitey's ice cream?"

"Of course! Doesn't everybody?"

"I thought I'd stop and pick up a quart. Do you like black cherry?"

"My favorite."

"Mine, too. I'll see you in twenty minutes."

***

Amy hung up the phone. *Best friend…now? What could you possibly be thinking?*

She tidied up, combed her hair into a bun and applied lipstick. Appearances were important, especially when you meet someone's best friend.

No matter how hard she tried, nothing would hide her red and swollen eyes. Her disappointment renewed the tears, ruining what little success she'd achieved in hiding her pain and suffering.

CHAPTER 43

Friday, July 9th

Brian made a bee-line for his house to pick up a few things before heading to Whitey's for ice cream. While waiting for his quart of black cherry to be hand packed, he checked out the shirts that were on sale. On a whim, he bought a red T-shirt. On the front in white, it read, "If I can't have a Whitey's malt, I'll get the shakes." He hoped Amy would like it.

When Amy answered the door, Woodford wasn't ready for what he saw. Her eyes and nose were red and stains from recent tears streaked down her delicate cheek bones.

"Amy, are you okay? I could come back another time."

"Don't be silly. I'm fine. Besides, you're the perfect medicine for what ails me. A shoulder to lean on."

Amy looked around the yard. "I thought you were bringing your best friend. Couldn't he make it?"

"He's here. I just left him in the car in case you didn't want a meet and greet."

"Of course, I want to meet him. Brian, you were awfully rude to make him wait in the car. Sometimes you men are so thoughtless. Get going! I don't want him to wait another minute. Honestly, if he's your best friend, I'd hate to be your enemy."

She followed Brian out to the car and was nearly bowled over when Barker leaped out and took off running around the yard.

Brian could hardly contain his mirth when he looked into Amy's eyes. "Did I forget to tell you my best friend's my dog?"

"Brian Woodford, you are a scoundrel!"

"Come here, Barker. I want you to meet a very special lady."

Barker bounded over and stood quietly next to Woodford, his big eyes begging for a treat.

"Amy, this is Bob Barker, and he's been my best friend for the last five years. Barker, I want you to shake hands with the nice lady."

Barker raised his right paw, which Amy solemnly shook.

"It's nice to meet you, Mr. Barker. Welcome to my home."

Brian followed Amy onto the porch and sat next to her on the swing. Barker lay at their feet chewing on a rawhide bone that Brian brought along.

"Amy, Barker is a great watchdog, and I'd feel a lot better if you'd let him stay here the next couple of days until we get this case wrapped up. I've brought his food and a few of his toys. He's housebroken, but if you want you can tie him up outside. I guarantee you if he starts barking he'll scare away any intruder."

"Barker, you'll be inside with me. I won't lock you up and leave you outside by yourself like this rogue of an owner who calls you his best friend."

The evening was cool for July. A perfect night to relax on the porch and enjoy their ice cream. Amy loved her Whitey's shirt and put it on right over her blouse. She placed her arm inside his and lowered her head upon his broad shoulder. Amy raised her chin and stared into his deep brown eyes and whispered tenderly, "Thank you."

Time passed by without a spoken word. Their closeness said it all.

Brian felt like he could stay there for hours, but finally uncurled himself and softly kissed Amy goodnight. He bid his farewell, said some words to his trusty dog, before heading home with a heavy heart and a thousand wonderful thoughts running through his mind.

Before crashing, he sent text messages to his team reminding them of Lizzie's visitation on Sunday and her funeral at 11:30 on Monday at Our Lady of Victory Church. He was a C-and-E Catholic (Christmas and Easter), and it had been many a year since he'd participated in the sacraments. He hoped the walls wouldn't crumble when he walked through the front door.

CHAPTER 44

Saturday, July 10th

Woodford chuckled out loud as he read the Quad City Times lead story, "WOODCHUCK ARRESTED FOR LOCAL BURGLARIES." He read the whole article to see if anyone from his department leaked information to the paper, but they hadn't, so that was good. What wasn't good were the editorials concerning the fears of the Davenport community over the rash of murders and robberies. This bothered Woodford greatly. It was his department and his duty to keep the city safe. Hopefully, the arrest of Billy the Woodchuck would calm the community.

The weather finally took a turn for the better after the oppressive heat they'd suffered through the past month. Brian wanted to stop by the morgue and talk to Ball and also check on Tillie, but first, he needed to find out if Woodchuck's lawyer had stopped in to see her client. Woodchuck...he was going to have a real hard time calling him Billy.

By the time, Woodford reached his office it was almost 9:30 and he wasn't totally surprised to see Jane, Carl, and Frankie hard at work.

***

Jane got up at the crack of dawn and corralled Sue Hatfield before she started her shift at Emeis.

"Sue, I've been told you were Lizzie's best friend. So, what are you hiding from? Is it Billy Perkins? If it is, he's going to be in jail for a very, very long time."

Jane could see the look of relief come over Hatfield's face. The flood gates opened and Sue began sharing everything she knew concerning Billy, Liz, and all the other girls on East High's track team.

***

Detective Owens was checking into truck rentals because Ricky Porter would need something to clear out his house. Meanwhile,

Frankie was searching into Billy's life. His service and police records, plus anything else that might indicate what makes Billy tick.

Squid made a wisecrack about Woodchuck, just as Chief Angel walked into the office.

"Mornin', my stand-up comics. How ya'll doing this fine day?" His mimicking of a southern drawl was far from perfect, but worked fine for what he was about to say next.

"Good morning, Chief. Did you see the paper this morning?" asked Woodford.

"I did. But I've got some seriously bad news, kids. I released Billy this morning cause of your lack of attention to the fine letter of the law."

"WHAT?" they all echoed in astonishment.

"According to his lawyer, none of you have a license to hunt woodchucks inside the city limits. She also pointed out that woodchucks are out of season. And furthermore, none of you read him his rights in woodchuckese, so ain't nothin he said can be used in a court of law. Sorry, kids, you blew it."

Jane couldn't stop laughing while Frankie sat there and shook his head. *'What did my sister get me into?*

"Good morning."

They all spun around at once to face Kelly Daniels, the attorney for Billy Perkins.

"Chief Angel, Detectives Woodford, McCreary, Hawthorne and whoever this gentleman is. I am shocked that you find it amusing to belittle my client. Especially you, Chief, of all people. Don't you realize that woodchucks have feelings, too?"

"Enough," said Woodford. "Kelly, have you spoke with your client?"

"I have, and he's ready to plead guilty to the robberies, against my counsel. Woodford, my client would like to have a sit-down with you this morning concerning the killing of Liz Porter. He's ready if you are."

"Let's do it."

Kelly Daniels, Woodford, and McCreary entered the interrogation room where Billy Perkins waited. Daniels sat next to her client, Woodford across from them, while McCreary stood just inside the door.

"Billy, do you know Detectives Woodford and McCreary?

"Yeah, I talked to em last night."

"I'm not pleased with your act of stupidity, but it's a little late now to worry about that. I told them you were willing to plead guilty to all the Kwik Shop robberies even though I advised against it. Do you still plan on going against my wishes?

"Maybe. What am I being charged with?"

"Let's begin with your assault on Tamika Gaines," said Woodford. "That is a felony and will get you twenty to life in a state pen. Your robberies can add an additional twenty-five. Is that what you want? Of course, if you have a good lawyer and a judge sympathetic to your case, you could possibly walk away with maybe thirty tops. A lot depends on your past history. If you're a habitual criminal, you will probably get the max. But, I'm sure your lawyer has told you that.

"You are a good lawyer aren't you, Miss Daniels?"

She smiled and nodded. "Sure."

"I have no priors," cried Billy. "So, if I plead guilty what are you offering?"

"Well, Mr. Woodchuck, in your words...'Let's Make a Deal.' I've decided I'll drop all the robbery charges, including the felony assault *if* you plead guilty to the rape and murder of Liz Porter."

"Dammit, Woodford! I told you last night I didn't rape, and I sure as hell didn't kill anyone named Liz Porter! I'm not going to plead guilty to something I didn't do!"

"We'll get back to that."

Over the next hour, Woodford peppered Billy with questions about the robberies, his service history and coaching experience.

Daniels' frustration was boiling over. Billy wouldn't listen to a word of her advice and Woodford's constant berating of Woodchuck finally sent her over the edge.

"Woodford! Tie this up or we're out of here! Capiche?"

"Agreed."

"Billy, let's say I believe you didn't kill Liz. So, enlighten me. Why would you rob four stores in three days?"

Billy flipped stories like pancakes. First it was gambling, then it was an addiction to coke.

"I owe a local dealer ten grand," he stated, "and I was short two bills so why not rob a few stores." This was his final story and he stuck to it.

Woodford didn't believe this fairy tale any more than his gambling one. What he did believe was that Billy hired a professional hitman to get rid of Liz because of his lewd behavior, and to kill Nana and Amy in case Lizzie already spilled the beans. Who knows who else might be on the hit list? Perhaps Sue Hatfield or Becky Ahlstrom, Lizzie's friends.

One thing was for sure, his take from the four earlier Kwik Shop robberies wouldn't come close to covering the bill to have three people taken out. However, gambling to earn the additional fee made extraordinary sense.

Woodford and McCreary stepped out of the room for a few minutes while Woodchuck and his lawyer discussed their options.

Upon their return, McCreary took charge of the questioning while Woodford stood in the corner and watched as his protégée went to work.

"Mr. Perkins, we caught you with your paws in the till, so to speak. Tamika Gaines wants to see your hide nailed to the wall."

Billie's lawyer barked out, "Detective, that's enough with the Woodchuck humor. Let's get on with it."

"Fine. Miss Gaines has reluctantly agreed to drop charges if you plead to the aforementioned charges of rape and murder. Which brings us to your relationship with Liz Porter. We'd like to hear your side of the story."

"Don't answer that!" Daniels yelled.

"It's a little late now, don't you think? There's not much to the story," conceded Billy. "I'm her assistant track coach and we had a great student athlete/coach relationship. Really, there's nothing more to tell."

"Do tell," said Jane. "I have it on tape that late last season you fondled Liz in the girl's locker room on more than one occasion.

And she was not the only girl whom you preyed upon. What do you say to that?"

"Billy, zip it!" shouted Daniels. "McCreary, do you have an eye witness or is this just hearsay? If what you say is true, surely someone would have come forward and reported it to the authorities. And that hasn't happened, has it?"

Jane took another approach. "Billy, last night you stated that you were in Chicago on the 4th of July weekend. You gave us the name and number of the friend you stayed with. But the name, number, and address don't exist. Would you like to try again, or will you just tell us more lies?"

"Detectives, I think we're through here. I need to consult with my client and we'll talk again on Monday."

"Ms. Daniels, before we depart, I want to add something to Woodchuck's thought list."

Just as Daniels started to object Jane interrupted, "On the 4th, a young girl in Chicago was slain in the same fashion as Liz. Identical. And what a coincidence that you just happened to be in Chicago on the same day. I don't believe in coincidences, Ms. Daniels, nor do I believe for a nanosecond that Billy can't remember who his friend is. If we're to believe one word about his trip to Chicago, we better have the correct info in our hands before you leave this office or there will be no lenience shown. Do you understand?"

Woodford stepped out from the shadows by the door. "Billy, I need to see your neck. Lift your chin."

"Don't do it Billy! Woodford, I need a minute alone with my client."

Daniels waited till the two Detectives left the room. "Billy, why would Woodford want to see your neck? Is there something that happened I should know about?"

"Lady, your guess is as good as mine, but there's nothing wrong with my neck." He tilted his head and pulled down his shirt. "See?"

Daniels walked over and opened the door. "You can come in now. Woodford, I don't know what your game is, but if it will clear my client of any wrong doing in the Porter killing, then have at it."

Woodford checked both sides of Billy's neck and shoulders. He considered making a wise crack about being unable to see anything because of the fur, but thought better of it.

"So, are we done here?" asked Daniels.

"Yeah, we're done for now."

Jane interrupted. "Billy, I still need the name, phone, and address of your friend in Chicago. If your alibi checks out, I'll see what I can do to help with the robbery charges. Lie to us again and I will make sure the full weight of the court comes down on you."

The two detectives left the interrogation room dejected. There were no recent scars on Billy's upper torso, so he could not be their killer. But, did he hire an assassin? That was the million-dollar question.

CHAPTER 45

Saturday, July 10th

Sergeant Squid Hawthorne returned to his desk during the interview of Billy Perkins. He was still miffed that McCreary took over his case, and now she was in the interview room instead of him.

Personally, he was not thoroughly convinced Billy killed Holly, Liz, and Hund. Pedophile, yes. But with no criminal history, he found it hard to believe the woodchuck could turn into a rabid killer.

That last thought got him thinking. Just because Billy didn't have a rap sheet, didn't mean he hadn't killed before. Perhaps he just never got caught. He logged on to the Behavioral Analysis Unit/National Center for Violent Crime. He limited his search to the mid-west, female, ages 15 to 35, throat slashed, stabbed and sexually assaulted with a foreign object, the last two post mortem. He hit send and logged off. Perhaps Billy's past history might reveal secrets of which they were unaware. If so, he wanted to find out.

***

The flotilla was that afternoon and the class reunion gang would be gathering soon to float down the Mississippi for a gorgeous day of fun and relaxation. The temptation to join his classmates was overwhelming, but Squid's aspiration to become a detective trumped his desire to join his classmates, even if it meant he'd miss the opportunity to spend a few leisurely hours with Mary Lou.

Besides, he would be with Mary Lou at the dance that evening, and if all went well, they would end up at her place with a nice bottle of wine, soft music, and a full moon to keep them company. He'd fallen head-over-heels the second he met Mary Lou. *If ever there was love at first sight, this is what it would feel like.*

Everyone else departed for places unknown, and he was tempted to follow suit when his desk phone rang. It was his buddy, Wally, from the impound lot.

"Squid, my man. You know that green Honda you've been looking for? They found it about three blocks from the Porter's place. We've got it down at the lot. Care to take a look? Or wait till Monday? Kelly's got the Jones fight on tonight and me and my gang thought you might like to hang out with us, that is if you ain't got nothing better to do."

"As a matter of fact, I just happen to have met this young lady that's stole my heart, and tonight we're going to sit under the moon and listen to some Jimmy Hendrix and share a bottle of wine. I'm telling yah, Wally, she could be the one. So, thanks, but no thanks."

"Damn. You've got to bring her over to the tap. I gotta see the chick that's finally put the hook into my man Squid."

"Yeah, right. Like I'm going to share her with a bunch of boneheads like you guys."

"Oh, man, you're breaking my heart. Look, I'll see yah when you get down here to check out the Honda, and you can tell me all about this girl of yours."

Before heading down to the impound lot, Squid gave Woodford a call. "Hey, boss, it's Carl. They found Hund's green Honda three blocks from the Porter's house. It appears the stalker that got away the other night was definitely our murder suspect. I'm heading over to check it out now. Care to join me, or are you busy?"

"You take it. I'm at the Porter's interviewing Amy and her mom. If anything newsworthy pops up give me a call. And Squid, you've been doing a bang-up job and I won't forget it."

"Thanks, boss!"

Hell, if he could get the girl and the badge, what a hell of a week it would turn out to be!

The Honda sat just outside the garage door. He checked in with Wally and waited restlessly while they towed the car inside. Squid, Wally, and his team of CSI investigators tore the old beater apart, bumper to bumper. The sixteen insurance identification cards, all in the name of Raymond Hund, were proof enough of ownership. Empty beer cans and candy wrappers told of his eating habits, but nary a print could be found to identify whom the last driver might have been.

Hawthorne was far from a Behavior Analysist, but common sense told him their suspect would need new wheels. After finishing up with the Honda, Squid returned to the office and phoned the Auto Theft Division to see if any vehicles were pilfered in the past twenty-four hours. There had been three. One looked promising. A Caddy was reported stolen from the Rhythm City Casino parking lot, just a half mile from the Porter's residence. For his taste, it was too much of a coincidence that somebody other than their stalker was responsible for the theft. An APB for the Caddy was already in place, but no results were forthcoming. He tagged it urgent and spent the next twenty minutes going over paperwork before closing up shop and heading home to get ready for the evening's festivities.

CHAPTER 46

Saturday, July 10th

Up to this point the Davenport East's class reunion was a smashing success. Old friendships were renewed and new budding relationships were beginning to flourish. All in all, a hearty two-thumbs up.

On this glorious Saturday afternoon, everyone looked forward to the flotilla down the Mississippi, which would be one of the highlights of the day's festivities. It began at the landing dock near the entrance to Credit Island. There were 23 boats including two small yachts, a couple of speedboats, and a handful of sailboats, but mostly fishing rigs of all sizes. One pontoon boat making the trip overflowed with daintily clad women, drunken sailors, and multiple coolers filled with any beverage the heart might desire.

After much deliberation, Bones decided there were too many risks for him to join the flotilla. Besides, that pesky Squid might show up and spoil everything. So, he watched as they pushed off and slowly began their trek down the Mississippi toward the laid-back river town of Buffalo, Iowa. He waited until the last boat was out of sight, then jumped into the Caddy and made his way south along Highway 22 to Buffalo Shore Park.

The sun shone brightly the whole trip and the unwise were slowly turning crimson red. A couple of gals decided to skinny-dip like they did during their high school days, and a few of the guys soon followed suit, or should it be said, suit-less. Mostly, they just laid back, soaked up the sun and drank their day away.

The smell of brats and burgers filled the air as the flotilla reached the landing docks in Buffalo in just shy of three hours. A few of the boats anchored offshore, their captains and crew enjoying one last swim on this beautiful July day.

Bones found a great spot to sit back and watch all the families relishing this gorgeous Saturday afternoon. Little did they know this day would haunt their memories for the rest of their lives.

As more and more people swam to shore and began preparing for the picnic, Bones took up his hiding place amongst the trees.

Mary Lou and Jackie Townsend were setting the tables, while Tim and Roger were priming the keg left over from the golf tournament the day before. Others were throwing Frisbees and horseshoes. A game of flag football erupted in the small field west of the river. Everyone was having the time of their life, except for Bones.

Just like that, he pounced, but grabbed a limb that stopped his forward motion. A young man collecting cans stepped out from behind a tent. Bones didn't think he was seen. At least the man showed little facial recognition that he spotted him. He sat back and took a breath and patiently watched and waited until the whore would be by herself, and then he'd pounce.

Jackie excused herself (too many vodka tonics) and rushed over to the row of porta-potties. Mary Lou finished setting the tables and went in search of her picnic basket, containing deviled eggs, chips and home-made salsa. Her donation to the picnic feast.

Mary Lou never had the chance to scream.

The cut was not as precise as Lizzie's, in fact it was downright sloppy by Bones' standard. Perhaps she'd turned her head at the last moment or he attacked from the wrong angle. None-the-less she would die, he felt sure of that. He let go of her hair as she dropped to the ground. He took a moment to see if anyone was near, but all were frozen in shock. So, he took the time to kneel and stabbed her not once, but four times. The whore would never make fun of him again. He stood, gave a quick look over his shoulder, used his pants to wipe the blood off the knife, then casually walked to his car and drove away.

Several members of the flotilla witnessed the savage attack of their friend but were too stunned to react, except to scream for help.

Don Jansen, the transient looking for cans in the trash bins, reacted first. He dropped his precious load of cans and rushed to the aid of the dying young woman. He tore off his raggedy old shirt and pressed it firmly against her neck, stopping at least momentarily the spurting of blood that drenched her bronze body.

A local yelled out he'd called 9-1-1. As it was, several by-standers called 9-1-1, including an inebriated Tim Cain. One by one members of the class of "96" circled their dying friend. Many crying, others in utter shock.

Jansen yelled for someone to bring him something clean that he could swap for his bloody shirt. A young kid came running up and handed him a beach towel. Slowly he peeled back the shirt, revealing the nasty gash, then quickly replaced it with the towel and re-applied pressure. "Can someone please help me put pressure on the stomach wounds?" cried Jansen.

The town's volunteer fire truck careened into the park five minutes later. Two paramedics hit the ground running before the big rig came to rest.

Don moved aside but continued putting pressure on the neck wound. "She's been slashed across the neck, and whenever I release pressure I hear air escaping." What he knew but didn't say was that the carotid artery was sliced in two. She would be dead before she ever reached the hospital.

They carefully rolled her onto her back and cuffed her arm. Her blood pressure was critically low. Her pulse rate was rapid, but weak and thready. Her breathing, shallow and erratic. She was in hypovolemic shock and needed to be transported immediately. They were just starting a saline drip when the ambulance arrived. The back door swung open, and two EMT's bounded out dragging a gurney between them. In less time than it takes to make a peanut butter and jelly sandwich, they strapped her body to the cot, loaded the gurney into the ambulance, and headed towards Genesis East, lights flashing and sirens screaming.

CHAPTER 47

Saturday, July 10th

Trent Buckley just set the receiver down on the last of the 9-1-1 calls when Squid entered the outer office on his way to picnic with Mary Lou.

"Carl, you need to contact your team. There's been another attack, out in Buffalo. The woman's still alive, barely, and in transit to Genesis East."

His face went white and he struggled to take in his next breath. *Please, God, don't let it be Mary Lou.*

Jane and Frankie heard the call on their scanner and immediately contacted Woodford.

"Boss, there's been another attack, this time out at Buffalo Shore. Same MO as Liz Porter. The victim's being transported to Genesis East as we speak. She's alive for now, but it doesn't look good. We're heading to Buffalo to talk with witnesses. The drunk who called in the 9-1-1 said the girl's name is Mary Lou. Isn't that Carl's girl friend?"

"It is. I just talked to Squid no more than an hour ago. I'll try and catch him before he finds out what happened. Keep in touch." He said a hasty goodbye to McCreary, and made a bee-line to the station.

Woodford stepped out of the elevator when he heard Carl scream. He tore down the hallway and came face to face with a hysterical Sergeant Hawthorne.

Trent looked up at Woodford. "I didn't know. I'm so sorry. I didn't know."

Brian took Carl's arm. "Let's go!" and the two took off on a dead run.

CHAPTER 48

Saturday, July 10th

Bones checked the rear-view mirror for the twentieth time to make sure no one followed him. They hadn't. He laughed at how easy it was to take a life. The whore practically walked into his arms. He regretted that time and circumstances didn't allow him to stuff something deep inside her, but seemed content he'd marked his kill.

His plan was simple. He'd hide out at the Porter family farm for a few days until things calmed down. Then he'd find some quiet time to spend with Amy and her mother.

The family farm sat a quarter mile off Highway 22. At this time of year, the trees surrounding the homestead completely hid the two-story home from view. It was perfect. He parked behind the horse barn and walked to the back porch. He did a double take to see if anyone followed. They hadn't. He walked in, set his brown paper bag down on the table, went into the bathroom and checked himself in the mirror. He didn't like what he saw, never did, and never would. What he did see was blood and lots of it. He went into the laundry room and found a pair of clean jeans and T-shirt. He threw his bloody clothes into a corner and went back to the kitchen. He sat naked in a tall backed chair and reached for his sack.

Tonight would be spent with his two best friends, Jack Daniels and Slim Jim.

A plan was forming in the back of his brain. It was a great plan, but timing would be everything. He might even get a good night's sleep. After a kill or two he usually did.

CHAPTER 49

Saturday, July 10th

When Brian and Carl arrived at the hospital they went straight for the emergency room. Brian guided Carl to a bank of chairs.

"Carl, why don't you stay here? I'll check on Mary Lou's status."

"Brian...wait. I know I just met Mary Lou, but I firmly believe I love her, more than any woman I've ever known. The second our eyes met we both knew we were meant for each other. Does that sound foolish?"

"No, sometime fate takes over. Let's pray that it didn't just play a cruel hoax on you."

Brian headed to the desk, showed his badge and introduced himself. "Do you have any information concerning the young woman who was stabbed out at Buffalo Shores this afternoon?"

"Yes. They just took her to the emergency OR. If you'd like, you and your friend can head back to the waiting room."

Thirty minutes later Dr. Oberhaus entered the lounge and motioned for Woodford to come over.

He whispered, "Brian, I'm afraid she's gone. We tried everything, but there was nothing we could do. I'm sorry." He pointed towards Carl. "Is he a member of her family?"

"No, Carl's one of my officers and Mary Lou's boyfriend. Can he see her?"

"Give me a minute, and I'll get the body ready."

Carl didn't even look up.

"She's dead. Mary Lou's dead, isn't she?"

CHAPTER 50

Saturday, July 10th, Buffalo Shore

When Jane and Frankie arrived in Buffalo they began by seeking out Tim Cain, who'd called in the 9-1-1, and other members of the class who might have witnessed the murder. Zoe Wilson just finished questioning Cain when the two arrived. Seeing Jane, Zoe came over.

"He's drunk. One time he tells me one thing and a minute later it's something else. I don't think you'll get anything useful out of this one, but I have a young man over here that helped out. I think you really need to talk to him."

Jane and Frankie approached the bare chested young man Zoe singled out.

"Hello, I'm Detective Jane McCreary and this is Detective Frank DeAngelo. Can we have a minute of your time?"

"I've told the officers everything I know, so I'd really like to be going."

"We understand, but we would much rather hear what you have to say than read what someone else thinks you said. What's your name?"

"Don Jansen. With an "E"."

"Don, can you tell us what happened?"

A look of embarrassment etched his face but he began with a little history.

"Detectives, I used to be a student at Northwestern University. My whole life all I wanted was to be a doctor. I'm smart enough, but not only did I have my schooling to contend with, I also worked full-time just to make ends meet. The closer it came to graduation, the more I struggled. There were never enough hours in the day. A fellow intern gave me some pills that helped for a while. Then I needed something stronger and he was happy to oblige.

"The police ran a sting operation and I got caught up in the middle of it. The university expelled me and no other colleges would take a chance on a druggie. I lost my job, my friends, and my dignity. Around that time, I remembered something my mom said. 'When all is lost, talk to God.' You know what? He listened. I'm off drugs and I've got a solid job. It isn't much, so I collect cans, a nickel at a time. Someday those nickels are going to get me back on my feet and I'll make something of myself, God willing."

Don continued, "Anyway, that's why I was here today, to collect cans." He twisted his body and pointed a finger. "I was over at that barrel, the red and blue one, when I saw this man come out from behind that tree over there. He walked straight up to that gal, pulled out a knife, and sliced her from ear to ear, and then bent down and started stabbing her. I took off after the guy, but when I got to her body I knew she'd die if I didn't do something fast. I tried stemming the flow of blood until the ambulance arrived. But, I'm afraid it was too little too late. That poor girl never had a chance."

Jane looked around to see who else was available to question when someone tapped her on the shoulder.

CHAPTER 51

Saturday, July 10th

A very loud and boisterous commotion was coming from the emergency room and Woodford went to see what was causing the racket. As he reached the doors, Jane and Frankie burst in, with Mary Lou close behind.

Carl rushed over and pulled Mary Lou into his trembling arms.

"I...I thought you were dead!" He held her at arm's length and stared into her eyes. "But, you're alive!"

Mary Lou lowered her head, "When I saw that...that awful man stab Jackie I dropped behind the picnic table and hid. It scared me so much! I did nothing. I didn't even try to help my friend. I curled up into a little ball and cried."

"Oh, Mary Lou, it wasn't up to you to save your friend. I'm just so grateful you saved yourself," sobbed Carl.

Like Carl, everyone was dumbstruck, but recovered quickly to join in with hugs, kisses, and jubilant celebration.

Then came a somber moment when it struck everyone that it was Jackie Petersen who'd been murdered. She had been the target all along. The witness, Tim Cain, who'd reported the victim as Mary Lou, needed to do a lot of explaining, but that could wait until another day.

The team gathered in the lobby and made plans for the rest of the evening. Jane and Frankie decided to head up to Tillie's room, while Brian went looking for Coroner Dr. Ball. Mary Lou needed a change of clothes and no way was Carl going to let her out of his sight any time soon. A lot still needed to be discussed before their day ended, so all agreed to meet at the Village Inn on Harrison Street in an hour. The dance that night was all but forgotten.

***

Tillie was wide-awake when Jane and Frankie arrived and thrilled to see them.

"Jane, guess what? My memory's returning! Not everything, but I remember a lot."

"That's great! You sound fantastic! Is everything healing okay? What about your eye sight?"

"Dr. Oberhaus says I'm his best patient ever. He's so happy with my recovery that he's going to release me on Tuesday. Isn't that great?"

"That's incredible! And I suppose the first thing you're going to do is go out and run a mile."

"No way! Seven miles! Remember I've got the Bix to run in a couple of weeks."

"Hold on there, young lady!" Dr. Oberhaus exclaimed as he entered the room. "You'll do no such thing, or I'll keep you locked up until the Bix is over."

"Oh, Doc, I'm feeling great! Seven miles is nothing."

"Jane, can you talk some sense into that thick skull of hers?"

"Don't look at me. You're the expert. Besides, that thick skull saved her life."

"Since I'm the 'expert', why don't you two step into the hall while I do a quick check of this young lady's noggin."

Minutes later Oberhaus stepped out of the room and closed the door behind him. "Detectives, I've never seen a patient recover so quickly from trauma as Tillie has. Even her mental state has done a 360 since she began remembering details of the attack. Technically, I could release her today except I'm afraid she'd overdo it and end up back in here. Jane, talk to her. She respects you."

"I'll see what I can do, but I won't make any promises she'll listen."

Jane opened the door and stuck her head in. "You decent?"

"Sure, come in."

"Tillie, you look like an excited kid on Christmas morning. What's got into you, girl?"

"My mind is clearing, and the fog is lifting. I still can't remember what his face looks like exactly, but I do remember his hair was long and straggly. I'm pretty sure he also sported a mustache and beard. I vaguely remember stabbing him with my keys, but that part's a little fuzzy. Dad tells me he threw me into the creek, but I don't remember any of that. I must have passed out, because the next thing I remember is being here in the hospital."

"Speaking of your parents, where are they? I'd like them to meet Detective DeAngelo."

"Dad said they were going shopping for a new camera and phone as a thank you for Dusty saving my life." Her face suddenly turned a brighter shade of pink. "Jane, did you see the bear and flowers Dusty gave me?"

"Yes, I was here when he brought them. He's a real hero in my book. And quite the looker if you ask me." She gave Tillie a little wink that made her blush even more.

Suddenly, Tillie went quiet as if she'd seen a ghost.

"Jane, I have a question that's been bothering me a lot. Why didn't he kill me? I know he killed that other girl, so why not me?"

DeAngelo cut in, "Our killer is a psycho. Something triggered in his brain that set him off. It could be that Liz reminded him of someone. Or maybe she said something that got him riled. We might never know what makes him tick. His mind is in constant turmoil and something is driving him over the edge, but that something is not you. It's not how you look or act. You were just in the wrong place at the wrong time. You probably startled him and he attacked, not thinking, just reacting. He's sick, but you are not the cause of his sickness. Do you understand?"

She nodded. "Jane, would you and Frankie come back and see me before I go home. *Please*?"

"As long as you put it that way, how could we resist? And who knows what you might remember by the next time."

CHAPTER 52

Saturday, July 10th

Before visiting with Dr. Ball, Brian called Amy and gave her a short synopsis of what transpired that afternoon.

"Oh, Brian, when will these slayings ever end?"

"Only when we catch this low-life, and hopefully that will be soon! I know you're upset, but would you like to join the team for dinner? We all need some time to process what's happened and just hang out with one another. Maybe it would take your mind off things for a little while. Do you think Nana would like to join us?"

"No, she went to bed early. But, I'll let her know you asked."

He didn't know how Jane would react to him showing up with Amy, but that was her problem, not his. After a short visit with Ball, Brian picked up Amy and shared a quiet conversation on their way to the Village Inn.

Along the way, Amy put her hand on Brian's shoulder. "There's more to this story than you're telling me, isn't there?"

"There is. Some details will be shared at the restaurant, but there are some that I won't disclose. They're too gruesome and I can't have you hurting anymore."

"Brian...did James do this?"

"No. Well, to be honest, I really don't know. For your sake, I hope not."

They arrived at the Village Inn to find everyone seated and sipping iced tea. He was pleasantly shocked when Jane smiled at him and welcomed Amy to their celebration party. Introductions were made all around and when they were finished, Brian pulled out a chair for Amy. The look of shock and surprise that appeared on Jane's face was hard to hide. Then she smiled.

Once their meals arrived, the conversation turned to yarns and anecdotes of their youth. When their waitress arrived later with a tray of desserts, it didn't take much arm twisting before they all agreed to have a piece of the Inn's sinfully decadent French Silk pie and a cup of coffee.

***

Frankie excused himself early, explaining he wanted to get back to Chicago and spend time with his family, but said he'd be back Monday for the funeral. Carl and Mary Lou were beyond exhaustion and exited soon after. Amy leaned over and whispered something to Jane, and the two excused themselves.

As time ticked by, Brian began sweating bullets. *What could those two be talking about? It couldn't be good. No, this is not good.* He was panicking like a schoolboy on the playground surrounded by bullies. He felt sure he was going to break out in pimples.

Jane and Amy returned to the table, all smiles.

No, this was not good, not good at all.

"Jane, I'm so glad we got to know each other under better circumstances," Amy said. "I had a great time tonight and thank you. I'll remember what you said," she said with a wink.

The trip back to Amy's remained painfully quiet. Brian couldn't ask what they'd talked about, but he was dying to know.

It was getting late and Brian realized Amy was exhausted. Tomorrow would be a long day. He knew there were so many things that needed to be done before the visitation. Thank goodness Nana lived with her, a crutch in a time of need.

When they reached the front porch, Amy thanked Brian for a wonderful evening and gave him a peck on the cheek. She whispered, "It was only girl talk." She left and went inside, closing the porch door behind her.

Before he left, he did a thorough search of the sides and backyard of her house. He walked across the street to check behind the bushes where the stalker hid two nights before. On his way back to his car he spotted movement out of the corner of his eye. Someone was following him. He reached for his handgun and realized he wasn't carrying, not even his ankle piece.

He spun around and dropped to a squat.

"Who's there?"

"Sergeant Greenwood, sir. I hope I didn't scare you. I've been walking the neighborhood keeping an eye on the house when I saw someone lurking about. I didn't realize it was you, sir. Sorry."

"Sergeant, you're lucky to be alive. How long have you been on duty?"

"I've been patrolling the neighborhood by car for the last four hours, but my butt was getting sore so I decided to check out the area by foot. Things have been quiet except for one couple out for an evening stroll and some dogs howling at the moon."

"Keep up the good work, Greenwood, and have a good evening."

Woodford made his way back to his car and slid behind the wheel. His thoughts returned to Amy. It was so difficult to say goodnight for so many different reasons. Did she care for him like he did for her? Was he doing everything he could to protect her from James? And his last thought before starting his car...is it possible she could still love him after all these years? He hoped so.

He slammed the car into drive and took off for the Circle Tap. A couple of cold beers and he would sleep like a baby.

CHAPTER 53

Saturday, July 10th

Carl and Mary Lou ended up at her place and shared a bottle of wine to celebrate life together. They cuddled up in an over-sized beanbag and took turns talking about their lives.

"Carl, tell me about your family."

"Oh, my. Where do I begin?" He tilted his head to one side and for a second was lost in thought. "I was adopted at two months by a couple who were childless. I never wanted for anything." Tears formed in his eyes. "They loved me like I was one of their own. Several years back they both died, just weeks apart. I lost two months of my life back then just staring at walls and drinking myself into oblivion. They were my only family and they were gone. Over time I came to realize my parents would want more from me than wallowing in self-pity.

"I did some therapy, and with the help of an old friend, signed up for the police academy. Now, what you see is what you get."

Mary Lou sighed, "Thank you for sharing. That must have been difficult."

"What about you? Any secrets you want to share?"

"Nothing so personal. You could say I lived a typical mid-western life. Two loving parents and a brother that lovingly tortured me every chance he'd get. I got married right out of high school and six months later I gave birth to a healthy six-pound baby girl. At nineteen, my loser of an ex packed a few things, slammed the front door on his way out, and hasn't contacted me since. I guess we all have some kind of skeleton in our closet. For the last ten years, I've been working as a secretary in the mayor's office. I enjoy the work, but I think I'm missing out on so much more that life has to offer."

She messed up his well-groomed hair and gave him a passionate kiss on the lips. "Do you know what I mean?"

"Are you asking me to marry you? Because if you are the answer is an emphatic, NO! If anybody's going to do the asking it's going to be me."

Silence ensued, but spoke volumes. The two settled back in their chair, entangled in each-other's arms, contentment etched upon their faces.

***

Jane turned on the television when she got home and watched the better part of Cool Hand Luke. She cracked opened a bottle of wine and called her parents. Her dad was an early to bed, early to rise type of guy and could be heard snoring. Her mom stayed awake putting the finishing touches to a watercolor of a child cuddled up in her mother's lap. They talked about her younger brother Tommy, who was stationed in Afghanistan. "He should arrive back in the States sometime near the end of the month. I'm planning a get-together for family and friends. I hope you can make it," begged her mother.

They talked a little about the murder cases, but her mom hated what she did for a living and began to nag about finding a safer job. Of course, there were always the comments about not having a boyfriend and would she ever get married and have babies. Her mom continued to nag until Jane finally interrupted.

"Gotta go, Mom, phone's beeping. Give Dad my love but save some for yourself." It went that way every time she called, but she called anyway.

***

Woodford ended up having more than a few beers at the Circle Tap and closed down the bar. For some reason he couldn't get to sleep. The murders, of course, were on his mind as well as Amy. Amy stayed on his mind a lot the last couple of days and he really liked the idea of renewing their romantic days. He didn't want a one night stand, but someone who might want to spend the rest of her life with him and fill the gap left by the death of his wife, Carmon, five years earlier.

His daughter Samantha never forgave him for her mother's death.

He remembered that afternoon as if it was yesterday. It was a nasty winter's day, and even though the roads were snow covered and icy, he insisted they go visit his father at the nursing home. They hadn't been to the home for weeks and he'd felt guilty. The fact that his dad was in the fifth stage of Alzheimer's and couldn't remember him or his family didn't make him feel any less guilty when he missed his weekly visitations.

On the trip home, a dump truck slid through a stop sign and T-boned their Malibu, killing Carmon instantly. The day Samantha left for college was the last day he ever saw his daughter. He talked to her on the phone occasionally and sent presents at birthdays and Christmas. But it was strictly a one-way relationship and he would do anything to make it right. If only he knew what that something was.

***

Frankie made it back to Chicago in time to kiss his little girls goodnight. Then the fights began. There was never enough money. He was always gone too much. They needed a new washer and dryer. Why hadn't he fixed the garage door? She was tired of being mother and father to the girls, etc. etc. He loved his twin daughters and wouldn't hurt them for the world, but how much longer could he put up with this hateful woman?

He grabbed a cherry Popsicle from the freezer and aimlessly walked to the spare bedroom where he'd spent every night for the past two years.

***

Bones struggled with his usual nightmares, so he pulled himself out of bed and went to the kitchen and thought about his plan. He needed a squeaky-clean alibi, or at the very least a patsy, and he knew just the man. He always had a plan and a back-up plan. So far everything was working just fine but that still didn't keep the nightmares away.

CHAPTER 54

Sunday, July 11th

Woodford slept in late, even for him, and didn't give Amy a call until 8:30. He wanted to check up on Barker to make sure he'd been good and also see how Amy was doing.

"Good morning, Amy!"

"Brian! You sound like you just woke up. Did you stay out late last night?"

No sense in lying. "Yeah, it was a late night. Couldn't sleep. I kept thinking about you and my daughter, Samantha. And of course, these murders are driving me crazy."

"If it helps any, Barker was a perfect gentleman. He slept at the end of my bed and didn't bother me until I stirred this morning. Brian, how can you afford that dog? He would eat me out of house and home within a month if I let him! I filled his bowl this morning and when I came back into the kitchen ten minutes later he begged for more. Those big puppy dog eyes are hard to resist, so I gave him another helping."

"You're spoiling him. He'll never want to come home. Which is one of the reasons I called. I'm coming over in a little bit and take him for a walk. You're welcome to join us if you'd like."

"I'd like that very much but Nana and I have a ton of work to do before the visitation, so I'll have to pass. But, I have a favor to ask and I hope you accept. Would you sit with me at the funeral Mass tomorrow?"

"I'd be honored, but shouldn't Nana be the one sitting beside you?"

"Of course. Nana will be on the opposite side. In case you haven't noticed, I've become very fond of you in the past few days. And if I haven't missed my guess, you care for me, too. I need your strength and support to help me through these last few hours before I say goodbye to my Lizzie. Will you sit with me?"

"If my sitting next to you will ease your pain or give you strength, then I'll be there. Have you talked to Nana about this?"

"She's the one who encouraged me to ask you. Surprised?"

"Yeah, very much so. I'll be over in a few minutes to pick up Barker and we can discuss arrangements for what I'll need to do."

***

Jane ran out the door by 6:45 A.M and proceeded to Our Lady of Victory for seven o'clock Mass. She usually sat near the front on the right-hand side. As she neared her usual spot, a man reached up and tapped her on the shoulder. It was Dick Silvermann, his wife Donna, and Tillie. Tillie beamed from ear to ear and looked great. Her bruising and swelling disappeared with a little help from her mom and Cover Girl. More importantly, her nose was perfectly straight. Jane scooted past Dick and Donna, giving each a hug, and settled in next to Tillie.

***

Mass began seconds later so Tillie needed to wait to tell Jane all the exciting news. After the last song and the procession of priest, deacon, and servers to the rear of the church, Tillie was about to burst. "Jane, Jane, I get to go home tomorrow! Doc let me out to go to church but I need to go back for a few tests on Monday. Then I get to go home. Isn't that great news? I get to go home! And guess what else? I remembered what the guy looks like. If I saw him again I would know him. Oh, and guess what? Dusty wants to take me to the movies and out to eat, and..."

"Tillie, slow down and catch a breath. Give Jane a chance to say something," Donna chided.

"You're right, Mom. I'm sorry. It seems like I've been locked up in the hospital for months and it feels so good to be outside again."

Jane grinned. "Tillie, I'm so happy for you! Everyone has been so worried. To look at you now you'd never know how much pain and suffering you went through. Will you be going home to Fort Dodge or to your apartment?"

"My parents want me to go back with them, but I'm going to stay here. I may not win the Bix but I want to run anyway."

"Ladies, why don't we all go out for breakfast," suggested her dad, "and then you can talk all you want."

"Jane, will you join us, pleeeese?" begged Tillie.

"I'd love to! How could I ever say no?"

***

Mary Lou gently pried herself out of the beanbag and tiptoed into the kitchen. She started a pot of coffee and then hurried to the bathroom for a quick shower before Carl woke up.

Carl was still sound asleep when she came back into the living room. She slid into the beanbag, crunched up into a little ball and stared in wonderment at the wonderful man lying next to her. She loved his dark brown curly hair and his deep-set eyes. She thought, *You would never call him a gorgeous hunk, but definitely ruggedly handsome.*

Their love-making that first night was fantastic, but just cuddling together last evening was special...no, extra special. They talked about anything and everything and he listened and cared for what she said. If ever there was love at first sight, this was it. She hoped he felt the same way.

Carl began to stir, so she slipped out of the beanbag and silently made her way to the kitchen and started making omelets and hash browns, just like her mom used to make.

***

The smell of coffee and the sizzle of bacon was more than Carl could stand. He rolled out of the beanbag, stiff and sore, but happier than any time he could ever remember. He went to the bathroom, splashed water on his face, and then followed the heavenly aromas to the kitchen. He snuck up behind Mary Lou, wrapped his arms gently around her small but curvaceous waist, and softly kissed her on the neck. "Good morning, beautiful."

"Dave, is that you? No, you sound more like Roger. Or, I know, Sam. Yeah, Sam. Good morning."

Carl gave her a love pat on the bottom and spun her around.

"Oh, I'm sorry, what's your name again?" asked Mary Lou.

He pulled her in close and held her tightly, never wanting to let her go. The eggs were beginning to scorch, as were the hash browns.

"See what you made me do? I never burn my eggs." She took the food off the burners, turned around and kissed him until their lips melted together.

Carl pulled apart. "Mary Lou, there's something I need to say before we continue like this. I don't think this relationship is going to work and perhaps I should leave now."

"What? But I thought you really liked me!"

"I do, but you put the toilet paper on the roller the wrong way."

She gave him a playful punch in the arm, then took his hand and led him into the bedroom.

CHAPTER 55

Sunday, July 11th

Amy and Nana were preparing to leave for the visitation when Brian arrived to pick up Barker for his walk in the park.

"Brian, I apologize, but between my enormous grief and getting myself mentally prepared for the visitation, I just don't have time for pleasantries."

Brian appreciated her need for solitude, so he gathered Barker's things and slipped out the back door for their daily walk.

They agreed that Brian would take Barker home and then join Amy and Nana for the private gathering of family and close friends later.

Brian cut their walk short so he could shower and change and make it to the funeral home by noon. When he arrived, the parking lot was already packed and people were streaming across the street to pay their last respects. The student body from East High turned out in masse. Each team wore its colors to show unity, love, and respect. It was almost more than Amy could handle and tears formed, bitter sweet tears, a mixture of joy and sadness. It meant so much, just knowing how much her daughter was loved.

Around 5:00 P.M, the last of the visitors finally left, leaving only a handful of relatives and closest friends. Amy asked if everyone would step out of the room. She needed a moment alone with her daughter.

Amy slowly walked over to the casket, knelt down and placed her right hand softly upon her daughter's shoulder.

"Hi, baby girl, can you hear me? I have to go soon but my heart will stay with you. I packed it full of memories, love, hugs, and kisses, so if you ever feel alone reach in and take a handful out. But don't worry, it will never go empty. I'll put more love in each and every day. One last thing before I go. I renewed a friendship with an old flame. He's strong and compassionate and seems to care for me very much. I wish you could have met him. He's special, just like you. Bye, bye, my darling. I'll miss you more than you'll ever know."

Amy stood, took one last look at her beautiful little girl, and left the room.

A few of her friends and family stopped by the house, but after an hour Amy excused herself and retreated to her room. Her heart was broken and she didn't feel well enough for small talk.

CHAPTER 56

Monday, July 12th

Woodford's team along with the Silvermann's, Tillie included, sat as a unit to show their support.

The funeral Mass began promptly at 10:00 A.M with Brian sitting next to Amy as promised.

Six of EHS's senior football players were pallbearers. The show choir sang several of Lizzie's favorite songs. Two of EHS's staff did the readings and relatives served as Eucharistic ministers. Father Charles gave a touching and memorable eulogy that brought tears to the whole congregation. The church was packed to overflowing with so many young people that it caused Amy to sob tears of joy to know her daughter was so beloved.

As the funeral Mass ended, Amy rose to leave. Without warning, her knees buckled. Woodford grabbed her about the waist before she fell to the floor.

Amy was completely overwhelmed.

***

The loneliest walk ever? A mother following her child's casket.

***

The caravan of vehicles stretched over nine blocks as it slowly weaved its way across town to Mt. Calvary cemetery.

The hillside behind the viewing tent overflowed with East High's red-clad mourners desperately trying to hear the final words spoken of Lizzie's love for track and music.

***

They were midway through the service when Tillie broke down. She squeezed Jane's hand, "That's him! That's the man who beat me!"

Tillie nodded towards a large man peering through pine branches of a nearby tree.

Jane gave Sergeant Hawthorne a poke. "That man behind the tree. Tillie thinks it's her attacker." Hawthorne slowly backed out of the crowd and circled around until he was directly behind Tillie's assailant.

***

"James Porter, it's the police!

"Don't make any sudden moves. Spread your legs and put your hands behind your head."

James knew his number was up, so with a deep sigh, he bit his lower lip and did what he was told.

Detective DeAngelo cuffed James and roughly shoved him towards Hawthorne's car. Placing his hand on James head, he unceremoniously thrust him into the back seat. Carl read Porter his rights and asked if he understood. Between cusswords, flying spittle, and his head banging against the window, Porter swore he'd get even. But he never acknowledged their request for understanding.

The trip to the station was quiet except for the static of the police radio and the grumbling of Porter as the plastic cuffs cut into his bleeding wrists.

***

Amy couldn't help but notice James being taken away. She gripped Brian's hand, "Is it over?"

"Yes, he won't bother you ever again."

However, in the back of his mind, he prayed. *If only it proves to be true.*

The service for Liz continued uninterrupted.

***

After the ceremony, most everyone gathered at Our Lady of Victory parish center, where the ladies of the church prepared a wonderful luncheon.

Jane introduced Tillie to Amy. The two hugged as if they'd been best friends their whole lives.

Eventually the crowd thinned, leaving a few helpers, immediate family, and Amy's newfound friends. She invited everyone to the house, but Jane declined. She needed to be at the station to interview James. Tillie grew tired as the evening progressed, so with little fanfare, Donna and David with Tillie in tow, bade their farewell. At the door, they caught up with Mary Lou and offered her a ride home, which she readily accepted.

Brian, who'd stayed out of the lime-light, worked his way over and gently placed Amy's hand in both of his. "Amy, I'm sorry. I wish I could stay, but duty calls. I need to interview James. I'd love to stop by later and share some private time. Would you mind?"

"Oh, Brian, you've been a pillar of strength and such a wonderful and kind man. How could I possibly refuse?"

They shared a long and tender embrace, after which Brian kissed her softly on the forehead and waved farewell, with a solemn promise to spend time with her that evening.

CHAPTER 57

Monday, July 12th

James was fingerprinted, photographed, and placed in Interrogation Room B. Two hours later, Brian and Jane strolled through the door.

"Good Evening, Mr. Porter. I'm Detective Brian Woodford and this is my second, Jane McCreary. You were a very difficult man to locate. So, thanks for showing. You saved us a lot of time.

I understand you've retained your own council. Will he arrive anytime soon?" Silence.

Woodford wasn't about to mess with this scumbag a minute longer.

"Mr. Porter, I suggest you listen very carefully to what I'm about to say. You've been identified as a person of interest in a crime in which a young lady was grievously injured on Tuesday, July 6th. Can you grasp the severity? James, you are going to be charged with attempted murder. We are also prepared to charge you with two counts of aggravated assault on one of my officers.

So, I hope you have a great lawyer, because you're going to need one."

"This is bullshit!"

"The man has a voice!" exclaimed Jane. "Any other insights you wish to share?"

***

Randy Walker, one of Davenport's most ruthless lawyers, violently pushed the holding door open and strutted into the room, exuding an air of superiority.

"Porter, that's enough! Woodford, excuse us. I need a moment alone with my client."

If you looked in the dictionary under 'scum of the earth' you'd probably find an image of Randy Walker. He was as dirty as any of his worst clients and the scourge of every judge in the Scott County judicial system. There's no line he hadn't crossed, no dirt he hadn't slung. Anything to secure the freedom of his clients. Over the last thirty years, he'd done it all.

Outside the room, Brian pulled his team into a tight circle. "Guys, it's time to cross every 'T' and dot every 'I'. This dirt bag is not going to slip through our fingers."

Walker signaled through the one-way mirror for the detectives to re-enter.

"Woodford!"

The sniveling little weasel couldn't wait to pounce on his favorite prey. "I see you still harass the innocent citizens of this fine city. And Jane, you look so hot. Why don't you quit this piss ant job? I can offer you so many fringe benefits. You'd be crazy to refuse."

"That's enough, Walker! Did Porter tell you what we're charging him with?"

"He did, and in his eloquent words...'It's bullshit.' According to James, all you're interested in is getting into Amy's pants. That's pretty low, even for you, Woodford."

Brian's face turned an angry, beet red. His eyes were the size of saucers and the veins in his neck bulged to the point of bursting. But, he kept his cool, took a couple of deep breaths and waited to hear what Walker was about to say.

***

"I've seen the charges, and since my client hasn't been booked I'll assume you have no proof James attacked a young lady on Tuesday. So, charge him with attacking your officer. We'll post bail and be on our way. You're wasting our time, Woodford."

"Not so fast, Walker. If you'd allow us to look at your client's neck and shoulder, we might very well make this all go away."

James was ready to agree, but Walker gave him an evil stare. *Zip it.* The message could not have been any clearer if Walker screamed it over a megaphone.

"Woodford, give me thirty minutes with my client and we'll give you our decision."

Jane came up and whispered into Woodford's ear, "Brian, mind if DeAngelo steps in? I'm meeting with a couple of East High students in 20 minutes. Hopefully I'll get some insight on Billy Perkins."

"Send him in. Let's see what he's made of."

"Thanks, and good luck. Keep your cool and try not to kill Walker before we get our case to court."

Thirty-five minutes later, Twiddle-Dee and Twiddle-Dumb re-entered the interrogation room and took their respective seats at the table. DeAngelo was introduced and took Jane's place next to the door.

"Several days ago my client had a cancerous growth removed from his left shoulder," said Walker. "He's still recovering and has a bandage covering the wound. At this time, we are prepared to give you the name of the physician to confirm what we're saying."

"Walker, I suppose you also have a bridge in the Florida Everglades you'd like to sell? Because I don't believe for one second this cock-and-bull story about a cancerous growth."

"Believe what you want, Woodford. So, are you going to charge James or let him walk? Because this interview is beginning to wear on my nerves."

"James assaulted one of my men. We will grant him the benefit of the doubt that he didn't know Hawthorne was a police officer, plus he did no permanent physical damage. So, we'll be charging him with a misdemeanor. However, tomorrow we are placing James in a line-up. If our victim identifies James as her assailant, not only will he be charged with the attempted murder of Tillie Silvermann, but will also be charged with first degree murder in the death of his daughter, Liz Porter."

From that point on the interview was basically a bust. Every time Woodford asked a question James would only answer, "I've been advised by council not to answer that question." But that didn't stop Woodford or DeAngelo from trying.

They were about to end the interrogation when the intercom buzzed.

"Sit tight gentleman, I'll only be a minute."

CHAPTER 58

Monday, July 12th

Jane talked to several of Lizzie's friends at the luncheon following the funeral and three agreed to meet with her around 6:00 at the station.

All three were waiting when Jane arrived. She offered each a soda and then escorted the first girl into an adjoining meeting room. Cassie Brown took a seat and began to squirm as she waited for Detective McCreary to begin the questioning.

"Hi, Cassie, there's no need to be nervous. Just be yourself. So, tell me a little about yourself and how you know Liz."

"Okay. I'm a senior at East High school, and did you want me to talk about my family and things?"

"Whatever makes you comfortable. But first, how old are you, Cassie?"

"I'm seventeen but will turn eighteen on September 4th. I have two brothers. One's in sixth grade, and the other is a freshman. Is this the kind of stuff you're looking for?"

"Absolutely. You're doing fine."

Cassie went on to talk about her parents, pets, and her likes and dislikes. The kid could talk forever.

"What about Liz? How well did you know her?" asked McCreary.

"Liz and I are best friends. Or at least we were until last year when she got interested in boys. I run track and cross country and sing in the choir. Liz and I were a lot alike in that way. That's why we got along so well. I've known Liz since second grade when my family moved here from Madison, Wisconsin."

"Cassie, let's talk about boyfriends. Do you know any of the boys Liz dated?"

"Are they going to get in trouble? Because I don't want anyone to get in trouble."

"It depends. Were any of these boys a lot older than Liz?"

"Liz liked older guys, especially seniors, and I know she went out once with a college freshman, but that didn't last very long."

"Cassie, this is personal and I promise I won't tell anyone who told me. Do you know if Liz was sexually active?"

"Do I have to answer that? I don't want anyone thinking badly of her."

"Cassie, it's very important to our case, and it might just help us find her killer. And I promise what you tell me is just between the two of us." *A little white lie, but if she found Liz's killer it would be worth it.*

"Liz told me once that she really liked this guy and they were going to go all the way at his place that weekend. I don't think she told me his name, but his parents were going to be out of town and they'd have the house to themselves. The next Monday at school she wouldn't talk about it and said it was none of my business. That's when we stopped being friends."

"Did Liz ever mention a boyfriend named Bill or Billy?"

Cassie lowered her head, "I don't think so."

"Cassie, this is very important. Please tell me the truth. Did Liz ever date Billy Perkins, the assistant track coach?"

Tears formed in her eyes. "I've got to go. Please don't ask again."

Cassie ran out to join her friends. They talked a moment, then as one, raced for the door.

"Please stop! I need to talk!" McCreary called out, but all three bolted down the hall and were gone.

McCreary was packing up when Cassie's friend, John, came back into the room.

"Detective McCreary, can I talk to you? It's about Mr. Perkins."

John Cartwright entered Jane's office and closed the door behind him. He looked back into the hallway to see if either of the girls followed. They hadn't.

"Please have a seat and don't be nervous. As I told Cassie, anything you tell me here is strictly confidential."

"You asked Cassie if Liz ever dated a Billy. The answer is no. But Billy Perkins, the cross-country coach, has been hitting on just about every girl on the track team. There are at least two girls I know who brag about having sex with him. Liz wasn't one of them. If I give you the names of the girls will you promise not to tell anyone? If the kids at school find out I squealed I'll lose all my friends, and who knows what they'll do to me!"

"Agreed. You said Liz never dated Billy, so are you saying he coerced her, perhaps forced himself upon her without consent?"

"That's what everybody's saying, but I really don't know for sure. There were a lot of rumors going around school near the end of track season about Billy and girls on the team. I think if you talk to Anna Towers and Jamie Witherspoon, they'll know more than I do.

"Please, Detective, don't hurt the Porters by bringing this up. They've suffered enough already."

Jane jotted down the names of the two girls John mentioned and thanked him for sharing.

"Google...phone number for a Clint Ashford in Davenport."

It took six rings before a scratchy voice answered.

"Ashford's, how can I help you?"

"Coach, this is Detective McCreary. I hate to bother you, but I need the phone numbers and addresses of two of your athletes."

"Detective, you should know I can't give that information out without permission from the principal."

"Coach, I have received reliable information that Billy was having sex with a couple of your girls. There are also indications that Liz was molested, and it's possible she wasn't the only one. I need to verify this information, and I believe these girls can give me what I'm looking for. If you won't give me their numbers, will you please contact your principal and get permission to release what I need?"

"Detective, I have your caller ID. Is this a good number where I can reach you?"

Three minutes later Jane was back on line with Coach Ashford.

"Here's the contact information you requested, Detective. If there's anything else you need I have permission to assist in any way possible."

McCreary thanked Ashford, hung up, and immediately dialed the first number.

Anna Towers was not at home, but the second girl, Jamie Witherspoon was. Twenty minutes later, McCreary banged on her door.

Jamie looked like she came straight out of Tattoo Illustrated. Plus, there were enough piercings to start her own consignment store.

Jane reminded herself, *One must not judge a book by its cover.* However, she was excellent at reading people and in this case, was positive that what she saw, was what she'd get. She was not disappointed.

"Miss Witherspoon, I'm Detective McCreary. Can we talk privately?"

"Detective, what's this about? I ain't done nothin wrong!"

Jane slid past her, entered the foyer and wasted little time getting to the meat of why she came.

"Jamie, I've been talking to several members of your track team and fellow students, and I keep hearing you're having an affair with your cross-country coach, Billy Perkins. Would you care to enlighten me about the accuracy of these statements?"

"That's really none of your business!"

Jamie pushed past McCreary and unceremoniously swung the front door open, slamming it against a potted plant. Leaves and potting soil flew everywhere. "I want you to get out...NOW!"

McCreary stepped out into the yard and then spun to face Witherspoon.

"Jamie, I am willing to keep this private. You know, woman to woman. Or, we can have a sit down with your parents. Your choice. Have a good day."

"Hey, wait. What do yah want to know?"

"Let's go back inside." Jane said with just a hint of a smirk.

They each took a seat on the couch. "Jamie, I'm not here to judge. This is a murder case and I have no options except to be blunt, so if I embarrass you, I apologize. Is there any truth that you're involved in a sexual relationship with Billy Perkins? Yes or no."

"Detective, I'm 18 years old. I can have an affair with anyone I choose."

"When did you turn 18?"

"Last week. Look, we love each other, and I was the one who chased after him."

"Did you know he sexually harassed several members of your track team?"

"No way! He's in love with me."

"Do you know Anna Towers?"

"Yeah, she's one of my best friends."

"I suggest you talk to her and see if you still believe that Billy is in love with only you. Jamie, this is between you and me. Not a word to Billie, understand?"

Jamie's admission of having sex as a minor would get the ball rolling. If she could get two or three more girls to collaborate Jamie's statement she could put Billy away for a long time.

Oh, Billy, Billy, Billy…you are in such deep shit. The boys in block A of the state pen are going to have a field day with you. Jane couldn't wait to get to the station and process what she'd learned.

CHAPTER 59

Monday, July 12th

While Hawthorne watched Woodford's interview with James Porter and his lawyer, a light went off and he rushed upstairs to his cubicle. Lying on his desktop was a fax, revealing information that would go a long way in solving their case. And he'd forgotten all about it.

He quickly scanned the fax before heading down to the interview room. He took a deep breath and punched the intercom button.

"Boss, I've got something you need to see NOW!"

Interruptions were a no-no, especially during the middle of an interrogation. But, this, this was worth any reprimand he might receive. This was gold.

***

Woodford exited the interrogation room, slammed the door behind him, and ripped the paper from Hawthorne's hand. "This better be good," he said.

He glanced over the fax, then slowly reread how Annabelle Porter was brutally killed.

As he re-read the fax for the third time, Woodford kept looking at Porter through the one-way mirror. Eventually, he walked in, took his seat, and re-read aloud the print-out he'd been given.

"James, who is Annabelle Porter?"

Porter started to answer, but Walker put a hand on his shoulder to silence him. "Woodford, give me a couple of minutes with my client."

Woodford turned his back and pretended to be out of ear shot. *Finally, they were getting somewhere.*

James turned to his lawyer and whispered, "Walker, I didn't kill Annabelle Porter. But I'm damn sure I know who did. And if this ties in with Lizzie's murder, I'll be a free man."

Walker gave it some serious thought. "Ok, Woodford. Let's get this fiasco over with."

James turned towards Woodford. "Annabelle Porter. Is that what this is all about?"

"Maybe, so talk."

"Annabelle was my aunt. She practically raised me once I became of school age. Woodford, she was a whore. Every minute I lived with that woman I wanted to kill myself. Years passed and when times finally got better I returned home to live out my teenage years with my family. Years later the QC Times reported Annabelle's murder."

"And why should I believe you?"

"Because I'm pretty sure I know who killed Annabelle. But first, what's in it for me?"

"Let's just say, *if* you can help us clear up the murder of Annabelle Porter *and* the slaying of your daughter, we'll drop all the other charges against you. And those are pretty big if's."

"I'm not confessing to anything, but yeah, we've got a deal. Detective, I have several cousins and at one time or another Annabelle took us all in. Times were tough. Annabelle had money and would help out our parents by looking after us. What our parents didn't know, and we were too afraid to tell them, is she treated us like slaves. Annabelle made us clean the entire house and do yard work and most of us were no more than five or six. Those were bad times, and I hated her guts. But my cousin Chip Porter hated her even more than me. He told me once, *'One of these days I'm going to kill that bitch. Mark my words, I'm going to kill her.'*

"Later in life, Chip went off to war, just like all us cousins. He did several tours for his country and when he returned he went straight back to the farm. By this time, Annabelle was old and feeble, but her wicked tongue never stopped wagging. Six months after his return someone broke into the house and sliced Annabelle from ear to ear, stuck a corncob into her cunt and for jollies stabbed her in the gut for good measure. Chip claimed to have been out of town visiting an army buddy, or so he said. They tried to convict him, but he was acquitted. As he walked out of the courtroom he looked at me and gave me a wink and a smile. Detective, after all that, danged if he didn't end up with the family farm."

"So, Porter, why spill the beans now and not back then?"

"Detective, they couldn't retry him. Double jeopardy. Besides, there was nothing in it for me." Porter gave a little cackle and sat up a bit straighter in his chair.

CHAPTER 60

Monday, July 12th

McCreary and DeAngelo took a road trip to Chip's farm. When they spotted the Cadillac Seville used in Jackie Petersen's murder, they called for backup.

A single light from a rear window greeted Woodford and the Swat team as they surrounded the Porter homestead.

Team A, led by Woodford, stationed themselves at the front of the house, while Team B, led by SWAT team commander Detective Arnold, approached from the rear. At exactly 7:10 the two teams stormed the house. The team executed a thorough search and, except for an orange tabby cat, no living presence was in the house.

The house may not have been occupied at the moment, but plenty of evidence existed to prove the current resident was indeed their killer. Bloody pants and shirt lay in one corner of the laundry room. A tactical knife lay on the kitchen counter and blood splatter covered the shower and bathroom sink. The Cadillac Seville proved to be the final piece of evidence Woodford needed to put out an arrest warrant for Chip Porter.

It was obvious they'd just missed Chip.

"Jane, take over here. Hawthorne, give her a hand. DeAngelo, you're with me. Let's go!" shouted Woodford.

As Brian climbed into his Chevy Impala he placed his throbbing head on the steering wheel for a moment and waited for the pain to subside. "Frank, is all this worth it? Are we making a difference in this world?"

DeAngelo didn't answer. He didn't need to.

"Frank, if James or his lawyer gave Chip a heads up, I'll charge both with accessory to murder and encourage the judge to throw away the key. I'm tired of being a step behind. This has got to stop!"

***

James didn't budge when Woodford rattled his cell door. Finally, he turned his head and opened one eye. "Did you get him, detective, or did he slip through your fingers?" His evil cackle echoed across the cell block walls.

Woodford wasn't about to be goaded again. "No...we didn't find Chip at home. But, I suspect you already knew that. Which is a shame. No one can collaborate your story, so you're mine!

"We'll see you in the morning. Sweet dreams."

"You can't do that, we have a deal!"

It was Woodford's time to cackle as the cell block door clanged shut, leaving James to ponder his future in the darkness of the night.

***

Brian returned to his office and sank deep into his chair. How could he have been so wrong? Everything pointed to James Porter as the killer. He had motive, opportunity, and his profile fit that of a killer. And Tillie identified him as her attacker. There were so many twists and turns in this case that his head felt ready to explode.

Time to call in the troops. But first he placed a call to Amy. She was anxiously waiting by the phone when the call came in. When she heard about Chip, she didn't know if she should be angry or relieved.

"Brian, are you sure it was Chip?"

"It looks that way, but there's still a lot that needs to be proved. James is locked up until tomorrow when he'll be placed in a line-up. Tillie is sure he was the one who attacked her. So, only time will tell.

"I know it's been a long and exhausting day, but James won't be harassing you tonight so try and get some sleep."

***

He went out to the lounge, put on a couple pots of coffee, restocked the fridge with cold drinks, ordered pizzas from Bills, and sat down at his computer to wait for his team's arrival.

CHAPTER 61

Monday, July 12th

Trent Buckley put out a call to everyone remotely involved in the Liz Porter murder case. One by one they trickled in. Dan Ball arrived last. None were thrilled to be there after the long and emotional day, but all knew what was at stake and were happy to oblige.

The first item on the agenda was to inform everyone about the life and death of Annabelle Porter.

Secondly, Brian wanted to make sure they were all on the same page. "We have three prime suspects. James and Chip Porter and our resident woodchuck, Billy Perkins. Let's put each under a microscope and see if we can eliminate one or more.

"Jane. I want you to lead off the discussion with what you discovered considering Billy Perkins."

First, Jane gave a tip of her hat to Sergeant Hawthorne for his diligence in researching the Kwik Shop heists. The least she could do. Second, congratulations were given to the officers who took charge and de-escalated a situation that could have easily turned into a blood bath at the hostage situation. Then she turned her attention to Billy.

"In my opinion, Billy "Woodchuck" Perkins mirrored the Clint Eastwood movie *The Good, the Bad, and the Ugly*. I think it's only fair we look at all aspects of Billy's life. From what I've been able to ascertain, Billy was an exemplary student throughout his elementary and high school years and a highly-decorated member of our armed forces. He dedicated himself to his coaching duties at East High School and is enrolled at St. Ambrose to finish off his teaching degree. All great attributes of a solid citizen, agreed?

"Now for the bad. According to Billy, he took on a life of crime to pay for a drug addiction, slash, gambling debt. You choose. In the past week he robbed four Kwik Shops, the last two at knife point. As you know, in the last robbery he took a hostage and we eventually captured him. He now resides here at the county jail.

"Zoe, you have a question?"

"If that's the bad what could he have possibly done that was ugly?"

"Well, earlier this evening I interviewed several students and track members from East High School and I found out that Billy Perkins is...a PEDOPHILE! Some students have stated that Billy molested members of the track team, one as young as fifteen. He also indulged in consensual sex with at least two girls who were juveniles. Is that ugly enough for you? It is my opinion, and mine alone, that Billy did not rob the Kwik Shops to raise money for his addictions, but to pay off an assassin to kill Liz because she was going to report what he'd done."

The pallor of death and lust shrouded the room. Everyone assumed James committed the crimes. Tillie identified him, didn't she? Then, evidence pointed its finger directly at Chip. It was his farm, his clothes, his knife, they were sure of it. And now Billy.

***

"I hate to throw another coal into the fire, but Detective Owens, can you shed any light on Ricky Porter?"

"Brian, as you know, Ricky was Amy's first husband. She divorced him and he left her everything in the settlement. It amounted to millions. It's speculated, but not confirmed, that Liz might be his illegitimate child.

"Steinman and I have been trying to dig into Ricky's past, but we've reached a dead end. We searched the internet and came up dry. Nothing...no birth certificate, no history of paying taxes, no driver's license, no credit cards, no nothing.

"We interviewed his second wife, Patty Sue Porter, yesterday. It was, let us say...'revealing'. We'll leave the finer details in our report. We needed to clarify a few points so returned today to find the house stripped clean. Not so much as a newspaper was left as evidence that the Porters ever resided there.

"We find it extremely peculiar that Ricky does not exist on paper. And when we did make contact with his wife, she disappears. Brian, we realize Ricky is not one of your main suspects. But we both heartily agree that if he is not, he most assuredly should be."

A few heads were nodding, either in agreement or because they were falling asleep.

Woodford's eyes were flickering in a gallant effort to stay open. "We've got two more suspects to discuss. Go refresh yourselves and be back in ten."

***

When they returned, Brian threw out the name of Chip Porter. "Who wants to take on our latest target?"

DeAngelo tentatively raised his hand. "I know I'm the new sheriff in town, but I feel I have a good grasp of what went down this evening so I'd like to give it a try."

"Annabelle Porter!" That got their attention.

"Annabelle was Ricky's mother and an aunt to James and Chip. She took in many of the Porters and others during hard times and, according to James, held a reputation as the town whore. Auntie Annabelle would literally use the children as slaves while in her care. She spurned hatred amongst the Porter children and years later was murdered. All evidence indicated that Chip was guilty. However, his rock-solid alibi helped to acquit him of the crime.

"Records indicate that her neck was sliced, she was raped with a corncob, and finally stabbed. Sound familiar? Fast forward to..." He looked at his watch. "Only a couple of hours ago. Damn, how time flies when you're having fun. Anyway, according to James, Chip inherited the farm and has resided there ever since.

"Jane and I drove out to the homestead, and subsequently found the Cadillac Seville used in the Jackie Petersen murder. Also, bloody clothes, a six-inch stainless steel combat knife, and blood splatter in the shower and bathroom sink.

"That was enough to put out an APB on Chip Porter. Nothing is proven, but very damaging. I wouldn't want to be in his shoes."

***

"Hawthorne!"

Carl's head shot up. "You want to take James? You graduated with him."

"Yeah, sure, of course, I... Yes." He took a deep breath and expelled the air. "James. As Woodford mentioned I graduated with James. Everyone knew him as the school's star athlete: quarterback, point guard, and anchor of the 4x100 on the school's track team. So, he most certainly could have run down Liz.

"All the accolades must have gone to his head because he terrorized anyone he didn't consider his equal, myself included. After time everyone learned to despise him, especially the girls, who he treated as inferior. I lost track of him over the years and just found out recently that he married Amy Porter and they bore a baby girl named Liz.

"For the past five days, we have been searching every possible data base and have come up with zilch for anything dealing with James' life, and I mean zilch. For all intents and purposes James never existed, just like Ricky. We know he slapped Liz, and treats Amy like a second-class citizen. I firmly believe James Porter is our murderer and I have no reservations in saying so. I believe he found out that Amy was unfaithful and bore an illegitimate child. In retaliation, he killed Liz and has been stalking Amy and her mother ever since.

If what I believe is true, Tillie will identify James tomorrow in the line-up and we'll put this case to bed."

***

"My, my, Carl," said Brian. "Do you think it's wise to put the cart before the horse? However, I tend to agree. I've heard the way he talks about Liz and the way he treats Amy. But, I sure wouldn't jump to any conclusions until I was absolutely secure of my findings.

"Okay team, that's it. Those are our four suspects. Two we have locked up and two are on the lam. Now that we are all on the same page, I want to hand out assignments so we can dig into their pasts. If there are no questions, take five, come back, and let's get to work.

CHAPTER 62

Tuesday, July 13th

"Team, tomorrow I'm going to put James Porter in a line-up at 2:00 P.M. That's fourteen hours from now, unless, of course, we can prove Chip was the killer. So, let's put our heads together and get to work."

Woodford checked his watch: 12:05 A.M. He'd caught his second wind and was fired up and ready to go. *Were the others?*

"Let's mix this up so we're not locked into one person. DeAngelo, go down and talk to Billy. Perhaps he's willing to talk. A night in jail will do that to you. Doc, see if you can dig up Annabelle's autopsy report. Let's see if James' memory is reliable or a figment of his imagination. Trent, pull up the records of Annabelle's murder. They won't be on film, so you'll probably find them buried in storage somewhere.

"Steinman, you and Owens hit the computers. Someone's deleted the lives of James and

Ricky. Put a square peg into a round hole. Even ghosts leave footprints if they're not careful. Okay, maybe not ghosts, but you get my point. Tandy, head down to your lab and see if you can pull any prints from the knife we found at the farm. Also, check for blood type, see if it matches Jackie Petersen's. God forbid if Chip used that knife to castrate a hog. Perdan, were you able to see the face of our killer in Tillie's pictures?"

"Sorry, boss. I tried every trick I knew, but couldn't enhance the images to get a clear look at the face. I'm still running them through facial recognition, not that it'll do any good."

"Jane, you and Hawthorne head back out to the farm and..."

DeAngelo came crashing through the door. His hands dropped to his knees. His breath came in large gulps as he choked out, "Billy's dead!"

"Did someone get to him?" gasped Jane.

"I doubt it, unless someone slit both his arms from the wrist to the elbow and left a suicide note. I found his note next to the bed on top of his bible. It read..."

'Detective Woodford:

I won't last a year in the pen, let alone life.

Tell Mrs. Porter I'm sorry.

Billy'

Jane was livid! "You're sorry, you're sorry! Sorry for what, you little puke! If you weren't already dead I'd go down there and kill you myself!" She'd put in so many hours to collar this creep and then he takes the chicken's way out. Jane collapsed into her chair. Her hands shook so bad she dropped the Pepsi she'd been holding.

Once she pulled herself together, the words '*tell Mrs. Porter I'm sorry*' kept running through her head. Over and over again. *Why was he sorry?'* She thought she knew. But with Billy dead it might prove to be hopelessly unattainable.

***

Brian and Frank returned to Billy's cell. They wanted to be there when Perdan and Tandy arrived. The pair were already dusting for trace evidence.

Perdan looked up over the edge of his glasses. "You're wasting your time, boss. This is as clear a case of suicide as I've ever dealt with. Go back and catch our killer. I'll finish up here."

James shouted from down the hall. "Did our little rodent get killed in a trap?" Cackle, cackle, cackle.

***

Back in the break room, Dr. Ball finished up with Annabelle's autopsy report and was preparing to share what he'd discovered.

About the same time, Trent Buckley trudged into the room, carrying two large dust covered evidence boxes full of log books, photos, personal insights, and trial summaries. Trent brushed off his shirt and coughed up dust. He plopped the boxes on the counter and proceeded to tell Woodford what he'd found. "I went online and found the name of the detective who worked Annabelle's case. His name is Antonio Hawkins. Do you remember him? He retired ten years ago and lives in Bettendorf. He wasn't happy I interrupted his beauty sleep. But, upon hearing why I called, he was more than happy to assist us in any way possible.

"The Annabelle Porter case turned out to be the last he ever worked. It haunts him to this day that he never solved the murder. He remembered the case well, even to where he stored the evidence in case someone ever called him in to assist. He gave me clear directions on where to find the boxes, and damned if they weren't right where he stored them.

"Trent, I want you to comb through Hawkins' notes," said Woodford. "Find out what he was thinking, not just what came out at the trial. Also, check to see if Annabelle had a rap sheet. James kept calling her a whore. Let's see if there's any substance to those allegations. Check to see if the names of any other Porters were mentioned in the transcript. Did Antonio share his thoughts on who he considered to be the guilty party?"

"He did. Antonio believed Chip appeared to be *'a couple of bricks short of a full load,'* but did not have the temperament to kill. He said during the interrogation Chip stated, *'If wanting to kill Annabelle is a crime, then I'm guilty as charged.'*

Trent continued, "Antonio said, even with that admission, he never felt right in charging Chip with murder. But, his hands were tied. He did seem pleased that Chip was exonerated.

"He told me he'd check in tomorrow and if we needed any assistance, he'd be happy to oblige."

Trent coughed up another dust ball and retrieved a Pepsi from the fridge.

***

"Doc. You were about to enlighten us on what you found in the autopsy."

"Brian, I think you'll find this very interesting. There are many characteristics basic to Annabelle, Holly, and Liz's deaths. But Annabelle's case is strikingly different. First, her body was covered with bruises on her face and rope burns around her wrists and ankles. Second, the slash mark on her neck, although similar to our other two victims, happened as she faced her assailant. Third, she incurred a stab wound post mortem. And fourth, the corncob was brutally forced into her while she was alive."

"So, what are you saying, we have more than one suspect, a copycat perhaps?" asked Woodford.

"OH, DAMN!" A light bulb went off in Doc's brain. "Brian, the autopsy indicated Annabelle was stabbed once. DeAngelo, Holly was stabbed twice. Right? Liz was stabbed three times and Jackie Petersen, four. We don't have a copy-cat, we have a serial killer who's tagging his victims. Why didn't I see that earlier?" said a very distraught Dr. Dan Ball.

CHAPTER 63

Tuesday, July 13th

Woodford poured himself a cup of black coffee and sat down at the head of the table. His right index finger made several circles around the lip of his cup before he finally addressed the group.

"I remember back during my Behavior Analysis class, our instructor laid the ground work for identifying a serial killer. The propensity for killing shows up at an early age, usually in a child who has been severely abused physically or mentally. Serial killers like the one we're dealing with historically begin by torturing or killing neighborhood pets. By high school, they become bullies and take out their anger on those they feel are inferior.

"Once they're old enough, many join the armed forces so they can take out their frustration and anger on the enemy and kill without repercussions. These men prefer hand-to-hand combat because they want to physically feel the kill. Eventually they come to realize the only way to silence the inner beast is to end the life or lives of all who caused them pain, real or imagined.

"If we apply those theories to our case, I can see Annabelle being the catalyst for driving any one or all of the Porters insane. Her subsequent death possibly soothed the burning fires within, but the ashes continued to smolder. They almost always do until the nightmares resurface once again. I believe our killer reached that point on July 4th when he took the life of Holly Jorgensen. Why he chose Holly is something we may never know, but for Liz, she was a Porter. She may have looked like Annabelle. It's reasonable to assume that Jackie probably knew our killer and at some point upset or embarrassed him, and that's why he took her life. Carl, you were a member of Jackie's class. Do you remember if any of the Porters dated Jackie?"

Carl scratched the back of his head trying to remember his high school days. "Boss, I hate to disparage her name now that she's dead, but she changed men as often as she did her underwear. And if she didn't like you she made your life miserable. Chip and James were in my graduating class. If I remember correctly, Ricky transferred to West his senior year. They were all good athletes and good looking, so I'm sure she dated all of them at one time or another. Hell, as I remember, she's the one who gave me my "Squid" moniker. Maybe you should put me on the list of killers."

Brian stood, and put his hand over his mouth to stifle a yawn. "Sorry, folks, let's take a break and think about what we just heard. Meet me back here in ten. Dan, got a minute?

"Have you received the results from the DNA we took from the keys and blood spill on the bike path?"

"No. But, check with Perdan. He might have heard something. It's only been a week. However, since we're dealing with a serial killer, chances are the FBI will move our case to the top of the pile. I'll get on it first thing tomorrow morning. I mean this morning."

It was 2:50 A.M by the time everyone returned to the conference room. Allison Tooney informed the team that Chip, Billy, and Hund served their country and all were highly decorated. "I've been cross checking their service records and at no time did they serve in the same unit, nor were they ever stationed together. I'll dig deeper once the rest of the world wakes up."

CHAPTER 64

Flashback to Friday, July 2nd

I'm going to stuff your head down the toilet and you can play with the rats.

Bones bolted upright, soaked in a cold sweat. Once again, his nightmares were sucking the life out of him, and he knew the time had come to silence the demons or silence himself.

He rolled out of bed and started pacing back and forth in his little room. He wished he could go to the house and take care of Nana and Amy once and for all. But after his last failed attempt, he knew their place would be heavily guarded. No, he would wait and plan, and when his time came, his demons would be no more.

His mind began to jump around, starting from his youth, where every living moment was hell, to the killing of Holly Jorgensen in Chicago.

He liked Chicago and would visit his friend, Andy Crombie, whenever he had a chance. On July 1st, however, he went there on business. Andy called and asked for a huge favor. His friend enjoyed banging a young girl on the side. One night the sex got out of hand and he'd slapped Holly. This was no sex game, it was a brutal attack against a defenseless young girl. She screamed in terror and threatened to tell his wife.

His wife's family was filthy rich, and the last thing his buddy wanted was to lose his cash cow. So, Holly needed to die.

Bones caught a taxi to Moline's airport and began checking out cars in the long-term parking lot. He found what he was looking for, a parking stub, time stamped that morning. Within minutes he'd jimmied and hotwired the car. He paid the attendant, exited the lot, and raced off for Chicago. His ever-present pair of dice were clicking in his fingers as the mile markers slipped by.

He'd spent the rest of Friday and all day Saturday stalking Holly, following her every move. One thing he'd discovered in his reconnaissance, Holly never locked her van and was even dumb enough to leave a spare key under the floor mat.

That Saturday night in the hotel room he experienced his worst nightmare ever. Sleep was not going to happen anymore that evening, so he opened his luggage, took out his knife and his pair of ivory dice. Carefully he honed the blade until it could split a hair. Satisfied with the results, he returned the knife to its sheath just as the sun broke above the horizon.

He took the dice, rolled them around in his hands, and tossed them to the base of a wall. Two fours! The gods were on his side. He finished off the last dregs of coffee and ducked into the shower. Thirty minutes later he hurried out the door as the early morning rays danced across Lake Michigan.

Traffic was light at this early hour and it only took twenty minutes to reach Jorgensen's apartment. Moments later he was rewarded as Holly took off on her early morning run. Just like the day before, she headed straight to the high school track and began doing laps.

He watched as she circled the track and became aroused by her long smooth legs and ample chest that bounced after every step. *No wonder his buddy stuck it to her every chance he got. Hell, if he didn't have a job to do, he'd bang her a couple of times himself.*

Chuckling with that thought, he took one last look, doubled back and hid next to a garage a few houses down from her apartment. The whore would die that day and she'd never see it coming. They never did.

CHAPTER 65

Tuesday, July 13th

The conference room tables were covered with old files, half eaten slices of pepperoni and sausage pizza, dirty coffee mugs, crushed soda cans, and a couple broken #2 pencils snapped out of frustration. The white board was covered with names, dates, circles, arrows, and scores of sticky notes, but no answers.

Brian grew more irritated by the minute, and it didn't help that Chief Angel stopped in twice demanding results. Instead of narrowing down the list of suspects, it had grown. Instead of two suspects, now there might be three or even four. There may also have been a hit put out on Liz Porter. He popped a couple of Tums and turned his attention back to his team.

"We've made a lot of headway this morning but there's still so much more to accomplish and so little time. Jane, you and Squid head out to Chip's house and go over it with a fine-tooth comb. That includes the barns and garage. When the sun comes up, talk to the neighbors and see what kind of person we're dealing with. Jane, I also want you to contact Tillie and make sure she's here by 2:00. Let's keep our fingers crossed that she identifies James as her attacker, or all this work will be for naught. Trent, I want you to check out phones and credit cards for Chip and Billy. Let's see what these two have been up to. Tooney, go on line and see if any of our suspects use a chat room, web site, or Facebook."

Woodford turned his attention back to Trent Buckley. "Besides the phones and credit cards, I want you to continue to sift through everything we have on Annabelle's murder. Check the detective's notes for anyone else who may have been a suspect. Get in touch with Annabelle's lawyer and see if he has a copy of an older will. Is anyone else suspicious that Chip got the farm and not her kids?" A rhetorical question that went unanswered.

"Frankie, when the cock crows, I want to interview James. Hopefully he'll give up the names of those who stayed at Annabelle's. We also need to find Chip and find out why he received the family farm and not Ricky or his sister. Perhaps after living in that hell hole they didn't want any part of it."

Brian walked to the window. It was still dark, but the city was coming to life. His team was great and he knew they'd all work through the night without him asking.

CHAPTER 66

Tuesday, July 13th

Carl stopped at the Kwik Shop on Locust and filled his pick-up while Jane went inside for two large big gulps of Mountain Dew. As an afterthought, she also grabbed two 5-hour energy drinks and a couple of Snickers. They were going to need all the caffeine and sugar their systems could handle.

When they arrived at Chip's farm, they saw a light on in the house and movement inside. Carl doused the car lights and parked down the lane from the barn. A pale blue Chevy was parked outside the house. The hood was still warm.

Carl approached the front door while Jane covered the rear. He took a quick peek through the living room window and saw one individual, possibly female, but it was too dark to tell. Carl tried the front door and found it unlocked. He slowly entered, gun drawn, and crept towards the living room.

"POLICE! HANDS UP! STAY RIGHT WHERE YOU ARE!"

Jane crashed through the back-door, gun ready.

"Don't shoot. It's me! Tooney!"

With hearts pounding, Jane and Carl lowered their weapons.

"What the hell are you doing here?"

"I came to pick up Chip's computer and laptop. Damn, you scared the hell out of me."

Jane and Carl assisted Allison in gathering the computers and helped carry them to her car.

The last twenty minutes spiked their energy level, so no need for the 5 Hour drinks.

The farmhouse had been built in the early 1900s. A two story, with five rooms on the first floor and four on the second. Jane took the upstairs while Carl searched the main level.

The second floor included three bedrooms and a bath. Jane started with the bathroom. It contained nothing unusual, just the bare necessities of a single man. Next, she checked out the first bedroom at the head of the stairs. The room was empty except for old furniture covered first with sheets and then years of dust. The large closet opposite the door held boxes of shoes, hats, and personal items obviously belonging to Annabelle. This was going to take forever.

Carl started in the den, rifling through desk drawers and searching the end tables. He found receipts for gas, feed, fertilizer, food, etc. The most recent receipt was from the past Monday at Farm and Fleet for a battery and work gloves. He flipped through the top batch of receipts, looking for dates that coincided with the murders. He found one for July 2nd from a BP gas station for $48 and another on the 4th for $43. Someone drove a lot of miles in two days. All the other receipts were what you would expect from a bachelor. Nothing stood out as being incriminating. This guy appeared to be leading a normal life, nothing like the picture Dr. Dan Ball painted.

While going through her third box Jane came across an old will for Annabelle that was dated fifteen years prior to her death. She scanned the document and was surprised but not shocked at what she'd found. A lot can happen over fifteen years, but the changes made to this will left a lot of questions unanswered.

***

Carl chose the sitting room next. Overly plush couches and chairs filled the room. There must have been at least a dozen throw pillows. Chip obviously didn't use this room, because the décor hadn't been changed in years and it was musty with some nasty smells. He checked the bookcases and under the cushions and decided to check the closet next. As he reached for the doorknob he stopped, his hand hovering over a dead bolt. *That's strange. Why would you have a latch on the outside of a closet door?*

He pulled back the bolt and looked inside.

***

At 5:00 A.M back at the station Brian checked his watch for the twentieth time. He hunched down in his chair and let out a long sigh. For the past two hours, he and Frankie used every search engine known to find information on the elusive Ricky Porter. Still nada. The same for James. At least he was in custody.

Dark rings were forming under their eyes as frustration and defeat etched their faces. Woodford reached up and gripped his graying hair with both hands and began shaking his head just as his phone went off.

"Detective Woodford? It's Carl. Jane and I made some fascinating discoveries out at the farm. These you need to see first-hand, the sooner the better."

While they waited for Woodford to arrive, Jane and Carl checked out the rest of the house. Now that they knew what to look for, the search became more productive.

Twenty minutes later, Brian, Dr. Dan Ball, and Frankie arrived. Jane met them at the front door.

"Gentlemen, welcome to hell."

Jane guided them to the kitchen where she'd laid out everything they'd found.

First, Jane showed them Annabelle's last Will and Testament and pointed out that the house, farm and livestock were to be left to the local animal shelter. Next, she pulled out two boxes of love letters, if you could call these vulgar requests by sexual deviants love letters. Then she produced journals filled with dates and names of men, hundreds of them, describing what they liked and how much they would pay and what she'd collected.

Brian scanned the list, and let out a slow whistle. He recognized the names of several prominent people in the community--judges, lawyers, politicians, and the like.

"Jane, what other goodies do you have for me?" asked Woodford.

Carl motioned for them to step into the sitting room and he opened the closet door. The inside reeked of stale urine, dried feces and mold. The walls were covered with crude crayon drawings made by young children. It was a jail, someplace to hide little pests when Auntie Annabelle entertained men at the house. Who knows how many years passed since the room had last been used. And yet it still bore the stench of hate and fear.

"Brian, there are three more closets like this, but this one's the worst."

Jane took them upstairs to the bedroom farthest down the hallway. Inside were five cots, nothing more than wood boards on top of boxes with a few blankets and small pillows. She searched this room and found little stashes of marbles, coloring books, dolls, small cars and blocks. Little things that meant everything to young children who feared they would be taken if found.

Jane felt so sad for these poor kids. "Brian, how in the holy name of God did no one know what was going on? It's no wonder they called her a whore and finally ended her worthless miserable life."

"Jane, she probably threatened them and maybe even beat them into submissiveness. Remember, these were young children. Once they got older and started to rebel she probably kicked them out."

"But why would Chip live like this?" questioned Jane. "Surely just being in this house reminded him of his past. That would drive me insane!"

"Perhaps when we catch up with him he'll tell us, but don't count on it. The memories may be too much for him to share."

The team spread out and covered the house once again, then the garage and barn. Carl checked out the old Ford F150. The gas tank was full, which probably would account for one of the receipts, but both?

The sun arose just as they were finishing their search. It was time to go home, take a cold shower, and then return to the office and see what the others found.

CHAPTER 67

Tuesday, July 13th

Even though they were supposed to meet at 10:00 A.M, everyone except Brian arrived in the office by 8:00. He had forgotten all about Bob Barker and arrived home to find the place a mess. Garbage was strewn everywhere. The large bag of dog food he'd just purchased had been ripped open. But the worst were the pee puddles and poop that greeted him at every turn. He wanted to get mad, but Barker's eyes were begging, '*Where have you been? I missed you.*' Instead of a shower he spent the next half hour cleaning up the place and then took Barker for a long and much needed walk.

After returning and indulging in a long hot shower, Brian called Amy. They talked for over an hour, covering everything from Billy and his suicide, to discovering the horrors at the Porter farm.

"Brian, I never heard of a Chip Porter or an Auntie Annabelle. Ricky and James never talked about their childhood. Now I'm beginning to understand why."

***

Now that the world was awake, vital information began filtering in and team members shared what they found.

Carl and Jane began by revealing to the rest of the team all the secrets hidden in Annabelle's house of horrors. They also announced they'd gotten in touch with Tillie and Roger Timberline, one of the classmates who'd witnessed the murder of Jackie Petersen. Tillie was coming in at 2:00 P.M for the police line-up. Timberline would follow fifteen minutes later.

Next Trent shared what he'd found. "The Caddy found at the Porter's farm was stolen four days earlier from the Rhythm City parking lot. Chip Porter owned two vehicles, a Ford 150 which we found at the farm and a Ford Ranger. I've put out an APB on the Ranger but nothing so far."

Dr. Ball checked in next. "Boys and girls, good news. The DNA tests on the blood and skin found on Tillie's keys is being analyzed as we speak. Hopefully by this afternoon a match identifying our killer should be made."

Brian stepped forward to pass on his latest news. "When I stopped by my desk a few minutes ago, I discovered a sticky note that informed me Ricky Porter is back from vacation and is coming into the office around 1:30. Needless to say, he was shocked when he arrived home and found it stripped clean. He actually called in and reported the theft. I'm sure he'll be equally shocked to find out that's not what we'll be discussing. Then, perhaps not. I also made contact with Bridget Porter Booth, Ricky's sister, who now lives in New York. She refused to talk about her childhood. According to her, '*Life as a child was too painful and she's paid too much money to shrinks so she could forget.*' But she added that if we catch Annabelle's killer she'd like to know who, so she could send him a thank you note."

Trent announced, "I've found no credit cards or phone numbers that would tie any of our suspects together. Chip uses his credit cards quite often but that's not unusual for a farmer."

Exhausted, DeAngelo got out of his chair and plopped down on the edge of the table. "First, I want to thank all of you for making my stay here so enjoyable, even though the hours are a bit more than I'm used to."

After a few chuckles and some nodding of heads, he continued.

"Earlier Brian and I dropped in on James and asked for the names of cousins who previously lived with Annabelle. James rolled over in his cot and politely informed us to go screw ourselves. I really hope he's our killer because I'd love to wipe that smug look off his face."

The team meeting began promptly at 10:00 and finished by 11:30. Everyone was exhausted and looking forward to cleaning up, and maybe even catching a little shut-eye before the interview with Ricky at 1:30 and the line-up at 2:00.

It was not to be.

CHAPTER 68

Tuesday, July 13th

At 11:35 a 9-1-1 call came in that a fisherman spotted a floater near the I-280 Bridge. Minutes later a second 9-1-1 call came in from a frantic woman whose daughter was grabbed at gunpoint outside their home.

The black and whites took the drowning victim, while Woodford and his team made their way to the Hale residence.

Mrs. Hale was standing in the driveway of her home when the team arrived. A host of friends and neighbors surrounded the distressed mother.

"Mrs. Hale, I'm Detective Woodford, and these are my partners, Jane McCreary and Frank DeAngelo. Could I have your first name please?"

"Mary, Mary Hale. I called a week ago and told you April was being followed. But no one took me seriously and now he's got her. I told you! Why didn't you listen?"

Jane placed a hand on the woman's shoulder. "Why don't we go inside? If it's a kidnapping he might be calling for a ransom and we don't want to miss the call."

"Detectives, we don't have much money! But, if he'll return April unharmed, it's his!"

Jane led a panic-stricken Mrs. Hale up the steps and into the house. It was a nice little ranch in a quiet neighborhood. The interior looked like it was decorated in early relative. It held nothing new, just comfortable old furniture that had been well cared for.

Jane was trying to calm Mrs. Hale down when Brian stuck his head through the door.

"Jane, can I talk to you for a sec?"

Jane stepped outside.

"I just received a call from the station. Someone spotted our suspect's van heading over the Centennial Bridge into Rock Island. Police have the Illinois side blocked off and as of right now it's a standoff. Our kidnapper is threatening to kill the girl, so keep mom here until the situation is under control. I'll keep you posted. Once I give the all clear you can bring her over."

The standoff between police and kidnapper reached the boiling point by the time Woodford and DeAngelo arrived on the scene. SWAT teams were in place on both sides of the bridge with snipers perched precariously high on the spans with instructions to shoot if negotiations failed.

Chief Angel and Captain Arnold from the SWAT team were discussing what steps should be taken next when Woodford arrived.

"Hi, Chief, Captain Arnold, are things as bad as they appear?" asked Woodford.

"Yeah, we've got a crazy. One minute he's going to shoot his hostage, the next he's got one leg over the railing threatening to jump and take April with him. He's on our side of the bridge so we're in charge. Any suggestions?"

"Chief, do you have a name for our kidnapper?" asked Woodford.

"He won't say. All he's asked for is to talk to one of the TV stations. We're afraid once he has the eyes of the nation on him, he'll take a shot at his fifteen minutes of fame and jump, taking his hostage with him. I'm up for suggestions if you've got one."

Frankie leaned in and said something to Woodford and then raced towards the camera crews forming at the foot of the bridge. Moments later Frankie returned with a microphone in hand and a KSTT hat and vest that he handed to Woodford.

"Let's hope this works," said Brian.

Woodford took off toward the middle span. With hands raised, his service piece taped to his back, and beads of sweat running down his forehead, Brian cautiously approached the kidnapper.

Captain Angel was livid. "Woodford, are you crazy?

Brian twisted his head around, gave the Captain a thumb's up and continued, one slow step at a time.

CHAPTER 69

Tuesday, July 13th

The body bobbed up again and this time the fisherman angled his boat alongside the floating corpse and grabbed the man's shirt. He steered his craft toward an opening between outcrops of trees and brush and pulled ashore where the police and fire crews were waiting.

The body was loaded into a waiting ambulance and taken to Genesis East where Dan Ball would get first crack at identifying the remains.

Ball placed the body on the center table and began dictating into a recorder. "Today is Tuesday, July 13th, and our drowning victim is a white male, six feet one inches tall, and weighing 198 pounds." Dan cut the clothes off the remains and slowly shook his head in disgust.

This was the fourth murder victim in less than two weeks! What kind of town had he moved to? He checked the clothes for an ID, but found nothing but a soggy receipt from Farm and Fleet. Details were difficult to make out, other than the total which came to $637.

Dan placed a call to Farm and Fleet and explained the situation. He asked the manager to check their records for anyone making a purchase of $637 in the past two weeks. They were more than happy to oblige.

While he waited, Dan continued to examine the body. He took his scalpel and cut a large "Y" into the man's chest, then cracked the ribs to expose the heart and lungs. He was particularly interested to see if any river water was present in the lungs. The minute amount he discovered was definitely not enough to consider this a drowning. His John Doe was long dead before being dumped into the river.

Dan spotted what looked like a bullet wound to the back of the man's head. His suspicions were confirmed when he extracted a 45mm slug from the man's brain.

Dan was in the process of getting dental x-rays and taking fingerprints when his phone rang.

The manager from Farm and Fleet called to say he found only one purchase for exactly $637 made six days earlier. A set of Goodyear tires had been purchased by one of their favorite customers, Chip Porter.

CHAPTER 70

Tuesday, July 13th

James Porter was part of a six-man line-up waiting for Woodford to return to the station.

Carl stalled for as long as he could as he waited for Brian and the rest of the team to arrive. Finally, he gave in to Walker's threats and bullying and brought Tillie into the observation room.

Tillie took a seat in front of the viewing window but was clearly upset that neither Woodford or Jane kept their promise to be there to guide her through the process.

"Carl, can't we wait until they get here?"

"I'm sorry, Tillie. Mr. Walker is demanding we get started or release his client. I'm not prepared to do that. You can do this, Tillie, there's really nothing to it." He explained the procedure and smiled at Tillie. "You'll do great."

Tillie looked at her mom and dad, and with a sigh said, "I guess I'm as ready as I'll ever be."

Carl punched the intercom button. "We're ready."

The lights came on and all six men were led into the room. One by one each man stepped forward, showed his profile, and returned to the line-up.

"Tillie, do you recognize the man who attacked you last Tuesday? Take your time. If you want we can have them step forward again."

Tillie took several minutes before she asked if number four could step forward.

"Number four, please step forward...turn to your right. Thank you, step back into line."

Walker slammed his briefcase against the wall and began screaming, "Come on, detectives, she obviously doesn't recognize her attacker, so let's end this charade."

"Be quiet, Walker. She can take all the time she wants. Tillie, do you recognize the man who attacked you?"

Tears were beginning to form in Tillie's eyes. "Carl, number four is definitely the man

I saw at the funeral. But...but up close I'm not sure he's the one who attacked me. He looks like him, but I can't say for sure he's the man. Sorry."

Walker was beside himself. "I told you my man was innocent! Let's get the papers signed so James and I can go have a martini. You guys are so pathetic."

"Walker, shut your trap. We still have another witness."

Tillie finally burst into tears as her mom, dad, and Zoe Wilson escorted her out of the room. It was all Donna could do to keep her husband, David, from returning and killing Walker.

"You haven't heard the last of me!" shouted David. "I'm coming for you, and that fancy title won't keep me from kicking the crap out of you, you son of a bitch!"

Walker took a step behind Hawthorne. He was about to say something, but Hawthorne pushed him in the chest.

"One more comment and I'll step out the door and let him at you. Understand?"

Once tempers settled down, Carl brought Timberline into the viewing room and they went through the whole process again. Sadly, the results were the same.

As much as he hated to do it, Carl released James to his smug lawyer. Paperwork still needed to be filled out and he would have to post bail for attacking Carl, but for all intents and purposes, James was a free man.

CHAPTER 71

Tuesday, July 13th

Woodford paused thirty feet from the gunman, took a deep breath, and summoned all the courage he could muster before resuming his walk.

"What's this bullshit? I asked for a frickin TV station, not some third-string disc jockey."

"Sorry, buddy, but I'm all you're going to get. So, what is it you want to tell the world?" Woodford extended the microphone, but in the blink of an eye the gunman took aim at Woodford and pulled the trigger. Shots echoed up and down the river. Brian grabbed his chest, dropped to his knees, and collapsed, motionless...

April screamed hysterically, her face and shirt covered with blood and brain matter. The sniper's bullet hit its mark squarely between the kidnapper's eyes. The impact of the shot sent the would-be kidnapper spiraling over the railing into the mighty Mississippi over a hundred feet below.

Police from both sides of the river rushed up to Woodford's motionless body.

Chief Angel was beside himself. "Brian, get up! I know you were wearing a vest. This ain't funny."

Brian rolled onto his back and gave the Chief a big shit eating grin, followed by a wince of pain. He reached up and plucked the bullet from his vest.

"Man, this hurts like...really bad. I might even have a couple of broken ribs. Have you no pity for a fallen comrade?"

Three medics rushed onto the scene. First, they checked out a hysterical April Hale. Frightened, but okay.

Woodford tried to stand but crumpled to his knees. "I think he broke my ribs."

"Woodford!" Chief Angel shouted. "I just received a call from the station. They're releasing James Porter as we speak."

Woodford pushed the medics away. "Over my dead body. Chief, tell them to hold that asshole. He's going nowhere."

CHAPTER 72

Tuesday, July 13th

Ricky Porter waited patiently for Woodford to return. He checked his watch, 2:30. "The hell with it." He could talk to Woodford another time. Earlier Ricky called Amy and expressed his condolences, apologized for not making the funeral, and asked if he could come over and share some memories of better times, if she was feeling well enough. Amy agreed. He told her he'd be there by 3:00 and he didn't want to be late.

James made bail and left the station almost five minutes before Woodford returned.

Jane dropped Mary Hale off at the bridge and rushed to the station to be with Tillie.

Ball was talking to Brian when Jane walked into the conference room.

"Woodford, you need to sit down and take a deep breath. Were you here when the 9-1-1 came in on the floater?"

"Yeah. Did they retrieve the body?"

"They did and you'll never guess who our floater was...Chip Porter! He'd been shot execution-style, once in the back of the head. Brian, that leaves Ricky and James as our only suspects and both just walked out the front door."

"Damn it, how long ago did they leave? We need to get their asses back in here, now!"

Brian dug deep into his pocket. His ribs were killing him and he struggled mightily to pull out his phone. He punched in nine and then paced back and forth waiting for Amy to answer.

Six rings and then the ever-familiar recording, *'No one's available at this time. Please leave a message at the tone.'*

Brian slammed his fist into his desk and raced for the door. "Let's go! Amy's not answering."

From the station to Amy's residence normally took ten minutes. Woodford made it in four.

They found the front door ajar when they pulled into the drive. Woodford, McCreary,

Hawthorne, and DeAngelo all had their service weapons drawn as they raced into the house.

CHAPTER 73

Tuesday, July 13th

When the doorbell rang, Amy was expecting to see Ricky, not the stranger standing before her. This man exhibited a crazed look about him that scared her to death.

Amy tried to slam the door shut, but the huge man blocked it with his booted foot and let out a jackal like laugh. He thrust his beefy shoulder into the door and stepped inside.

"What do you want with us? Are you going to kill us like all the others?" cried a hysterical Nana.

The man laughed, a mean snarling laugh. He grabbed Nana's arm, then Amy's, and dragged the two wailing women away from the front door and into the kitchen.

Nana started to say something, but he slapped her with his powerful right hand, knocking her back against the far wall.

Amy pleaded with the man, "Please, please, don't hurt my mom! Who are you? What do you want? Money? Anything! Just tell us what it is!" cried a hysterical Amy Porter.

"Your life," said the man as non-challant as if he were ordering coffee at the local bistro. He grabbed a razor-sharp butcher's knife off the counter and menacingly walked towards the two women.

Amy grabbed a chair and threw it at the man. He brushed it away like a pesky fly. Cups and saucers, potted plants, --anything Amy could get her hands on--she threw at her attacker. Anything to protect her mom, but nothing stopped him.

The man advanced, his blade singing as it moved from side to side. The third swipe caught Amy on the forearm, the fourth her breast.

As he prepared to thrust a fifth time, a deep voice boomed from behind him.

"Drop it!"

Ricky Porter charged the man, his full weight hell-bent on putting an end to the attacker's life. The other man struck first, slicing deep into Ricky's throat. The shocked look on Porter's face faded as he crumpled to his knees.

Silently, the stranger turned back toward the women, ready to finish the kill.

The first bullet ripped through his shoulder. The second, his spine. The last six were a waste of ammo, but all hit their mark.

The knife clattered to the kitchen floor. The big man crashed down beside it. He lay there face first in an expanding pool of his own blood.

Jane had never killed anyone before. She trembled as her pistol dangled from her right hand. Woodford felt nothing. They finally caught their killer and how things ended was meaningless compared to saving Amy and her mom.

CHAPTER 74

Tuesday, July 13th

The two bodies were left as they lay. Of greater importance were the health and well-being of Amy. The wound to her chest appeared superficial, but her arm was going to need surgery.

Amy was shaking and had to be helped into the den as she waited for the ambulance to arrive. Jane, Nana, and Woodford sat beside her, comforting and dealing with her wounds as best they could.

"I'm her husband. Let me through!"

James Porter pushed past the patrolmen who were stationed outside the house and barged into the den.

He showed no sympathy towards Amy or her mom, but instead turned his smug smile towards Woodford.

"I told you I didn't kill anyone. First my daughter, now my cousin. If you had any idea how to be a cop they'd still be alive. Now, get out of my house and let someone who knows what they're doing take over. And if I ever see you with my wife again I'll deal with you personally." He turned towards Amy, "See you later, bitch."

Woodford and McCreary initiated first aid while awaiting the arrival of the ambulance. Hawthorne and DeAngelo did a sweep of the house, but found it free of any other would-be attackers.

Brian thought his heart could never hurt as much as when his wife died, but today his heart was torn in two.

Nana packed a few of Amy's belongings and together with Woodford, followed the ambulance to the hospital.

As they sat in the waiting room, Brian swore that, somehow, he'd catch James Porter and make him pay for all the mental anguish he'd caused Amy. And he'd do it with or without his badge.

***

The ambulance was long gone before they turned their attention to the two dead bodies in the kitchen. Because Jane, Carl, and Frankie were involved in the shooting, they became bystanders as Detectives Owens and Steinman dealt with the would-be assassin and Ricky Porter.

Porter's murder was an open and shut case. They just needed to ship him off to the morgue and inform the next of kin, assuming they could find his wife.

The second body was another matter. Because police were involved in the shooting, great care was needed so that nothing was overlooked. McCreary, Hawthorne, and DeAngelo were questioned, a formality, since two eye witnesses could collaborate their stories. Woodford would give his deposition the following morning.

CSI Perdan and Tandy took great pains in photographing the body. Some lawyer would definitely question why anyone needed to be shot eight times...especially in the back.

Hawthorne was giving them a hand in turning their stiff when he dropped the man's shoulders and let out a gasp.

Recognition was complete. Squid confirmed the riddled body of the man laying before him was his best friend from high school, Bobby "Stinky" Rangel.

Suddenly, McCreary screamed, "Check his shoulder! Can you confirm that Tillie stabbed him?"

Hawthorne turned toward Jane and slowly shook his head no. "Can't tell. His shoulder was blown away by the first bullet. Maybe his blood type and DNA will match those collected at the crime scene."

CHAPTER 75

Friday, July 16th

It took some digging before they finally tied most of the puzzle pieces together.

Back when Bobby Rangel was a tot, Annabelle took him in to help his parents during tough times. Like many of the Porter children, Annabelle held him captive in one of the closets while she worked as a prostitute. Like the Porter children, Rangel would succumb to his natural instinct and pee himself. By the time Bobby arrived at school he'd reek and the other children would taunt him. "Stinky, Stinky, Stinky!"

Squid was able to fill in many of the missing pieces with the help of more amicable Porters. They were all guessing of course, but it made as much sense as anything. Annabelle died because... she was Annabelle. The third victim, Jackie Petersen, instigated the bullying and probably tagged Bobby with the nickname of "Stinky", just like Jackie tagged Carl with "Squid", a gangly, ugly creature. So, it was reasonable to assume, that's why Bobby felt Jackie needed to die.

But why did Bobby kill Liz Porter, Raymond Hund, Holly Jorgensen and Chip Porter? Or did he? There was a good chance that "Why?" probably died alongside him. Of course, there was still an outside chance there was another serial killer, or at the least, a copycat.

CHAPTER 76

Sunday, July 18th

Carl and Mary Lou were at the Circle Tap enjoying a platter of baby back ribs and fries. It might have been the ribs or his draft beer, but something jogged Squid's memory as to the conversation he and Bobby had shared.

Ring...Ring... "Woodford, it's Squid. Can you meet me at the station in ten minutes? Something's come up concerning our case."

"Spit it out, I'm busy."

"Sorry, boss. Not over the phone."

This was a bombshell and nothing less than a face-to-face with Woodford and McCreary would do.

Squid dropped his bombshell once McCreary and Woodford settled in behind their desks.

"We all remember Billy Perkins apologizing in his suicide note to Amy. But he never said why. Well, I think I know. When I went to my reunion at the Tap I ran into Stinky and asked him what he'd been up too. And I quote, *'Retired mostly. I pick up odd jobs here and there to keep me in pocket change.'*

"It makes so much sense. Stinky was working for Billy Perkins, and was doing a little business on his own," said Hawthorne.

Annabelle Porter...Holly Jorgensen...Jackie Petersen... Raymond Hund...Chip Porter, could they all be dead just because of MONEY and REVENGE?

As Woodford said since the beginning, "Follow the money."

Sergeant Carl "Squid" Hawthorne could almost feel the Detective's badge on his chest now.

CHAPTER 77

Monday, July 19th

Squid's enthusiasm was infectious and there was no denying the fact that Bobby "Stinky" Rangel had ample reasons for his killing spree. But, two plus two does not necessarily add up to four, especially when Woodford did the counting.

There was still one card out that had not been played. Until Woodford received the results from the DNA tests, his hand would not be complete.

After days of agonizing over not receiving DNA results from his murder scene, he finally gave the FBI at Quantico a call. His call was shuffled from one office to another, before finally being told to call back in twenty-four hours.

The next day yielded the same results.

Another day passed before they finally got back in touch.

"Detective Woodford," said a man with a squeaky, unsteady voice. "I'm sorry but there's no record of us ever receiving any blood samples from your department. Are you sure you sent them?"

If Woodford could have reached through the phone line he'd have strangled the little weasel and then he'd go after the person in charge. "Look again!" he screamed and flung his phone across the room.

Perdan and Tandy were at a loss and as was Dr. Dan Ball.

Samples were sent to the FBI on hundreds of occasions and never once had evidence been lost or misplaced.

What would he tell Amy, or would he tell her at all?

CHAPTER 78

Saturday July 24th

Early in the evening on July 24th, Brian was sitting on his back deck giving Barker a spirited rub down when the whole gang showed up. Time to party! Brian had already fired up the grill and several brands of beer were on ice. Steaks and lobster were the order of the day.

Amy's arm was healing well. It took nine stitches but luckily the blade did no permanent nerve damage. Nana was back to her old self, feisty as ever. Woodford sustained two fractured ribs from the bullet he took on the bridge. But, all in all, their bodies were recovering nicely. It would take a lot longer for the mental wounds to heal.

"Welcome to my home!" called out Brian, loud enough for the whole neighborhood to hear.

Amy took orders for food and drinks which she and Nana gleefully handed out to the team. Even DeAngelo returned for the festivities.

The party was in full swing when Tillie came bouncing through the back gate with a trophy and check held high over her head. That morning she won the Bix road race and set a personal best in doing so. Dusty tagged along behind her like a lost puppy dog.

Jane arrived last. She brought along Don Jansen, the young man who tried to save Jackie Petersen at Buffalo Shore. She'd cashed in some favors and managed to get Don into Palmer Chiropractic for the upcoming semester.

They'd seen each other a time or two. It wasn't a "thing" yet, but they enjoyed each other's company.

"Amy, have you seen Squid?" asked Woodford.

"He and Mary Lou were all googly-eyed and heading toward the gazebo. I think he's going to pop the question. Just a mother's intuition, don't you know."

Brian struggled to get out of his chair and gingerly walked down the cobblestone path, to the back yard. Squid and Mary Lou were in the gazebo as Amy thought.

Brian could see Carl down on one knee.

"Mary Lou, will you marry me?"

"Yes, yes, yes!"

Brian waited patiently until the two finished their long passionate kiss and embrace.

"Congratulations," Woodford called out from across the yard. "Carl, can I steal you away for a minute? You may have heard that Detective Owens applied for and was accepted into the FBI. That leaves our team a detective short. Know anyone who might make a great detective?"

Carl didn't bite. He just stood there shaking, unwilling to accept what might take place.

Brian paused for effect. Getting down on one knee, he asked, "Sergeant Carl Squid Hawthorne, would you be my newest detective?"

Carl wanted to scream, "Yes, yes, yes!" Instead he took the badge and handed it to Mary Lou. "Want to be a detective's wife?"

The party was a huge success, with Bob Barker being the happiest of all as he devoured the ribeye leftovers.

One by one each partier said their goodbyes, and when everyone was gone and the mess cleaned up, Woodford retired to his favorite chair with Barker at his side.

Looking up at the stars, he wondered if anything different could have been done. He hated to see anyone die, even the bad guys.

Amy walked up behind him and tenderly wrapped her arms around his broad shoulders. Brian turned his head and looked up into her deep green eyes, and smiled, a very loving smile.

CHAPTER 79

Nunavut, Canada, Sawtooth Range

The roar of the seaplane engine could be heard only by the native animals on this late July evening deep into the mountainous terrain of Nunavut, Canada. Its captain glided the plane into the cove, nicknamed Hive's Landing, and waited for the pier to rise before bringing it to rest. A large burly man stepped out of the plane and onto the dock. He waved the pilot farewell as the plane vanished over the trees and into the sunset.

It would be a year, maybe more, before he returned to civilization. The time had come for him to hibernate.

He walked up to the Hive and punched in his fourteen-digit code. Once the door opened, he stepped inside and typed the code in reverse. Seconds later the door silently closed behind him.

He was alone. The rest of the Hornets were in Syria taking care of business. Their return was unknown to him and he'd have it no other way.

He unpacked his belongings before proceeding to the vault. Once inside, he fired up the computer terminals and logged in. First on his agenda was to make several deposits in off-shore banking accounts. The largest, to the FBI agent who deleted all DNA info concerning the murder of Liz Porter.

Money could buy anything or anybody if the price was right.

Second, he broke into Davenport's database and deleted his prints and photograph. It was tricky, but nothing he hadn't done before.

Third, he needed to find a replacement for their lost comrade, Ricky Porter. He was one of the co-founders of the Hornets and a formidable leader. It would be a daunting task, indeed.

After several hours, he shut down the computer. As the last hint of light faded from the screen, he reached into his pocket and pulled out his dice.

The bones rolled across his desk and came to rest next to the keyboard...

A pair of fours.

Acknowledgements

First and foremost, I wish to thank God for the abundance of gifts he bestowed upon me. Creativity to develop this manuscript and the perseverance to complete my work are just two of the many gifts for which I will be forever thankful.

Thank you to Maggie Rivers, author and critic whose positive support and gentle criticisms gave me the confidence to push forward. Without her guidance, Bones would have been doomed from the beginning.

Viola Gill, my mom, is my number one fan who gently persuades me, "I could die before you finish your book." After each phone call, I'm back on the computer, rereading or editing. Thanks, Mom.

Julie Gill, the most loving and caring partner any man could ask for. I will be forever grateful for all the work and support you have given me.

To Kimberly Wuttke, there are not enough words of thanks for the editing you did on Bones. Your masterful critiques, technical corrections and positive reinforcements have encouraged growth in my writing career. I'm looking forward to working with you for many years to come.

To Jon Ripslinger, you are my hero for introducing me to Kimberly and for your enthusiastic support.

To Holly and Phil Perdan, Kyle and Doug Rick, Cheryl Wagner and so many others who were instrumental in making Bones a success.

To all my friends and acquaintances who were foolish enough to ask how my book was doing knowing full well they'd have to bear with me. A special thank you to my children, Jason, Jonathan and Janelle, who have supported me throughout this whole process.